Dedicated to Scott Baltisberger, my dad, whose old Conan the Barbarian comics introduced me to the amazing worlds of sword and sorcery.

This edition was written and self published by John Baltisberger.

Cover Art by Simone Tammetta
Edited by Lisa Tone

First Edition
www.kaijupoet.com

IBIRANU THE FLESHCRAFTER

CHILDREN OF THE GODS

JOHN BALTISBERGER

A SplatterPulp Book
From Kaiju Poet Publications

Chapter One

146 BCE

Ibiranu charged through the streets of Carthage, dodging debris as it fell from buildings. This was war. True war. Not the wars and battles he had fought before, not the sort of thing where he stayed locked in his tower reading entrails and casting curses and spells through polished silver or upon makeshift dolls. The young prince was lithe on his feet, with the knotted muscles of a man who had spent hours honing his body under the tutelage of true warriors. He was pale-skinned compared to other Carthaginians due to the other half of his training, long hours spent in the temple library studying rituals and spell work under the living God Baal Hemodiel. His eyes were mismatched by complete heterochromia, not that he would have known what that was, giving him one dark brown eye, common to his people, and one ice blue eye. These mismatched eyes were the blessing that had singled him out for tutelage from his master.

Though trained in combat, Ibiranu had never been in danger. He was the Prince of Carthage; he was far too important to be risked in a real battle. But now the dogs of Rome were at the gates, howling for blood. There was no separation between himself and the battle. He had a bronze sword, wet with the blood of the last soldier he had run into. Blood, blood was power. The young prince turned his mismatched eyes to the road ahead and slid to a halt. There was a group of Roman soldiers in his path; they marched forward, shields and spears at the ready.

He set his teeth. They might kill him, but he would damn himself before he allowed them to do so easily. Ibiranu slapped his hand against the flat of his blade, running his palm through the blood of his enemies. He would not be taken captive; he would not spare a single Roman. Raising his bloody hand to the sky, he pointed his sword at his enemies, chanting his prayers to Ashtarte and Baal Shemmon. He could feel the power flowing through him, channeled through his body from the gods. This magic was true power.

He extended his will, the blood on his hand steaming and boiling as he lifted the first wave of Roman soldiers into the air. They hovered there unsteadily, as if swimming in an unseen tide above the earth. With deft motions, his will seized their arms and legs, and with a smile, he wrenched his hand. Ligaments pulled and snapped as bones cracked apart and revealed the wet meat inside. The Romans were torn limb from limb. Their screams were music. Gore splashed to the streets and over the remainder of their phalanx. They tried to hide their fear. Their own oracles, their own mystics were things of gossamer power and trite tricks. They could not fathom the depth of Ibiranu's might, or his cruelty.

He turned his strange gaze to the surviving Romans. One of them, the one in the most ornate armor, was shouting for his men to not panic, to stay in formation, to not give in to fear. But Ibiranu would gift them a bouquet of reasons to revel in terror before he finished. He was a hero, no doubt, a leader. But now he would simply be an example. He reached into a satchel with his bloody hand and pulled out spell components, the grit and grease of reality. Bones filled with congealed marrow, dust from dead ruins, the scream of a tortured virgin. He spat in his hand, adding his own anima to the talisman of filth, and hurled it forward.

The wad struck the soldier's shield, and for a moment, relief crossed the man's face as nothing happened. That relief was fleeting as he was pulled forward towards the talisman. At first, he was simply confused, the sudden gravitational pull was more concerning than scary. But soon his face lit up with terror as his body was sucked into the tossed filth. His bones bent and cracked as every part of him was attracted to the marrow with the same savage force. His skin gave way first, ripping with a sickening squelch like torn wet leaves, and was sucked in. His blood never hit the ground, as it followed the skin, funneling through the air like a whirlwind of red to join the swirling vortex of his epidermis. Muscles, veins, and white lumps of fat were ripped from him to join the rest, but still he lived. Still he screamed.

His scream outlasted his body, the magic stripping him of all existence other than the sound of his anguish. With a cruel smile, Ibiranu spread his fingers; the neat little orb of matter that had been the hero exploded. Gobs of meat splattered against shields. Bones, teeth, and the harder bits of the dead man shot through flesh, skewering eyes, punching through throats, tearing out arteries.

Ibiranu laughed deeply, watching the Roman soldiers die. The magic flooded through his body, making him feel powerful, godlike. A moment later, that feeling fled, freezing in his veins as his laugh died in his throat. Overhead, the skies filled with the screaming roar of something massive. Darting for cover, Ibi looked up in time to witness the terrible shape of a black dragon flying over the city. A dragon could only mean the Romans were just a distraction from the true enemy. Baal Hemodiel had warned of the demons that would come, that the flood was inevitable. The Sheydim had come.

Ibiranu tore through the streets; it was undignified, but this was an emergency. Something in his primal animal brain broke at the sight of the reptilian overload that had flown above them. The only thought in his horrified mind was getting to the temple, to Baal Hemodiel's court. The might of demons would be terrible, but nothing could stand up to a god.

As he fled, he heard the sound of beating wings and screams. He could hear the fire roaring. Without Baal Hemodiel, this war was lost. But with him ...

Ibiranu steeled himself with the conviction that the Carthaginian gods were powerful, more than capable of dealing with this threat. With that thought in mind, he pushed himself forward, past the streets, up the temple steps, past the terrified guards to finally crash into the inner sanctum of the god.

"Master!" Ibiranu called out, his voice shattering the calm silence that existed only inside the temple.

There on his throne sat Baal Hemodiel, the god, Watcher of the world, Lord of Blood. The god stood at the sight of his disheveled servant and watched him with hundreds of ever shifting eyes that covered his bare body. Even standing, his languid blinking cockhead brushed the stone floor. It twitched, writhing between his legs, bumping against his three-balled scrotum, the only visible sign of his agitation. Ibiranu had seen him hollow out concubines and prisoners alike with the prehensile phallus he sported.

"Ibiranu." Baal whispered the name, but it filled the temple, peeling paint from the walls and rumbling through reality. "Why do you run?"

"Outside, lord, the Romans have brought demons. Demons and a dragon!" Ibi panted.

"And you assumed I was not aware?" One of Baal's many mouths lifted in a sardonic smirk. Another licked its lips, revealing yellowed canines.

"No … my god. No," Ibi sputtered, trying to control his own fear, his own awe. Humans were never supposed to be stuck in between gods and demons. "I merely though that … I could be by your side when the demons—"

"Lies." The word was a slithering serpent accusing Ibi of cowardice. "Instead of standing strong and denying the enemy entry into the holy of holies, you have scurried like a beast to my side in the hopes I would protect you." Outside the doors of the temple, screams could be heard as something terrible tore through the guards. "Why would I teach you power if you will not use it to serve me?"

Ibi stepped back from his god, horrified at the perfectly true accusations that Baal Hemodiel was leveling against him. What could he do? The enemy was at the gate, enemies that dwarfed his power, that eclipsed his own might, and now his only hope for salvation and life reprimanded him. It was too late to make a different choice now.

The doors of the temple flew open. A lone figure, cloaked in darkness, stood there, a demon of writhing shadows whose eyes burned with black flames against black skin. Behind him, the city of Carthage was awash in blood and flames. The shadows of gargantuan beasts and twisted demons roamed the streets, hunting down the people. Baal Hemodiel and the demon ignored it all.

"Little prince. Have you not tired of this game? How many times must we rend your flesh from your bones?" Baal spoke in the same sibilant serpentine whisper that wound its way through the temple.

The demon stepped forth, trailing dissolving wisps of smoke like shadow with every movement. Its hands, emerging from shadow-woven robes, twitched, six-fingered and too many joints, reminding Ibiranu of some terrible spider. Ibiranu was painfully aware that he stood between two beings of titanic power. He felt weak, and that feeling, more than impending death, terrified him.

Ibiranu attempted to flee then, darting to the side so at least he could get out from between the two monsters—and they were both monsters, he could see that now. He only wanted to flee before the two could actually come to blows. He took just three steps before a force gripped him, arresting his movement. Ibiranu let out a panicked yelp, looking back at the demon, but then realized it was not the demon who held him. Wrapped around Ibiranu's leg was the monstrous phallus of Baal Hemodiel, distended, still covered in angry, accusing eyes.

"You will serve me even if it is not as you choose," the god hissed. The cock dragged him back across the temple floor and, with a whip-like crack, tossed him in the air. The vengeful deity lifted his hand, and power channeled through him and into Ibiranu. The power was mutagenic, changing his body on a genetic level. He could feel his flesh writhing as he was forcefully remade.

Unseen by Ibiranu, the six-fingered Sheyd demon lifted his hand, his black lips moving as he intoned his own foul Sheyd magics. The demon's magic gripped Ibiranu and warred against the power of Baal Hemodiel. Far from escaping the worst of the confrontation, Ibi's body itself became the battlefield for the two immortal beings. He screamed with a mouth that was filling with savage broken canines, and then curved fangs, and then was toothless. The pain was like nothing the human mind could conceive as nerve endings were created only to be ripped apart, neurons firing through the meat of his brain in new paths simply to expand the frontier of agony that humans could experience.

Every cell of his body was a warzone in which the two titans exerted their unnatural will, each side winning and losing territories of flesh. Hemodiel was rebuilding him into something new, the demon was sapping his life and halting the process. His scream oscillated and fluctuated, changing pitch, tone, as his vocal chords were warped.

"Enough! I do not share my toys, Ashmandai, not with traitors such as you!" The god raised his voice, ending the challenge between the two beings. He swiped his hands through the air, recoiling his cock as he tore a hole in reality, a gaping maw of painful colors and discordant screams. With a dismissive gesture, the God discarded his servant, flinging the struggling and twisted boy through.

Chapter Two

Ibiranu fell through a void of unreality, all things twisting and turning around him in a vile kaleidoscope of sickening colors and painful visions, half hidden in a thick mist that rose and writhed around him. Unseen hands tore at his weak and ruined body, and visible ghosts screamed accusations as he tumbled his way through nothing, still screaming. Before his mind could even begin the task of comprehending the twisted realm he found himself in, he was out, shat through another hole in the unreality and into a new place. He screamed through multiple mouths as he emerged in a dark room and slammed into a shimmering pool of water.

Ibiranu panicked at first, flailing for purchase, gasping in water, and choking before he found the ground beneath him. The pool was not deep. He opened his eyes. Too many eyes. There was too much information coming into his human brain; it wasn't designed for this amount of sensory input. He was disoriented by the flood of sights that surrounded him. Ibi found himself in a palatial room crafted of black marble and gold. A swimming pool of crystalline water had broken his fall. It lapped at his skin, soothing that burning, squirming feeling that filled him. Pillars stood at regular intervals, set with guttering torches that set the world in strange, shifting illumination. Around the pool, women stared, beautiful women of every shape, size, and color. This was a harem; these were some lord's wives. Was this somehow a reward from Baal Hemodiel?

Ibi tried taking a step forward. It hurt. His entire body felt as though it had been drained of all strength and broken apart. He was dying; he wasn't sure how he knew that, but it was clear in his mind, as crystalline as the waters he now stumbled through. He could not die, not here. Baal Hemodiel had sent him to the pool filled with beautiful women. To die now would be to spit on that gift. He forced himself forward.

One woman, a dusky skinned woman with ringlet hair and kind green eyes, waded through the water towards him. She wore white linen robes draped over her in a way that hid nothing. Where the material soaked through, it clung to her skin. Had he not been in such exquisite agony, he would have been aroused; as it was, all he could consider was his pain and his desperation.

"Sirrah, my lord, you are hurt …" the woman began, reaching out to him to try to steady him. She recoiled as she saw his visage, the extra eyes and mouths; a dawning recognition lit her face as her concern was replaced by horror. But it was too late for her.

Ibiranu lurched forward, grabbing the woman by the throat. With words muttered from multiple mouths, he pulled the vitality from her. Her blood vessels shrank and then burst under her skin, covering her in growing bruises even as her flesh withered. Her eyes rolled in widening sockets before simply falling out of her skull. Within moments, her desiccated and hollowed corpse fell into the water.

Ibiranu stood taller, his wounds healing, his strength returning, replaced by the life of the woman he had drained. He was hungry for more. He felt like he could drain the life from every whore here, sup on their strength and feast on their flesh as Hemodiel had taught him. They were screaming now, fleeing. Ibi ignored their screams, pushing himself towards the edge of the water. As he passed under one of the torches, he looked down and, for the first time, beheld his new visage.

Half of his body, the left half, was normal and healthy, reconstituted by the life he had taken from the woman. The right—the right side was anything but human. Writhing tendrils of flesh like cilia unfurled from his flesh. His right arm split at the shoulder into three violet tentacles with puckering suction cups, each filled with a screaming mouth. Blinking eyes opened at seemingly random intervals along his shoulder and the tentacles.

His face was no better. Again, the left side was his visage, normal, healthy a handsome Carthaginian prince, albeit with an ice blue eye. His right side ... the skin was desiccated, pulled back in a snarl of twisted wriggling flesh and trembling muscles. Several eyes blinked from his skull; only his original two were human. The rest were reptilian or insect, monstrous and hateful. The teeth on that side were twisted as well, all fangs and gnashing tearing things incompatible with the human mandible on the left. He was a twisted monster

Under his armor, he could feel his body writhing, ignoring his commands. It was no longer his body, not entirely. He needed more strength. Several of his eyes swiveled up to see the last of the women fighting to get through the door. More, he needed more mana, more power. With power, he could undo this terrible curse. He lurched forward, pushing through the water towards them.

Magic was mathematics and physics and chemistry; it was all that and more. Spells were formula for reshaping the world, and spell components merely the ingredients necessary for such change. Now a different math ran through Ibiranu's mind. How much power could he expend to attain more from the women? It was an equation that had no definitive answer. Too many unknowns. How much life did these women have? How much could he drain?

He reached forward, clawing at the air between him and his quarry with the flailing tentacles. Normally, when he was healthy, tapping into magical power was no issue, but now? Now he could feel the pull of magic on his life force, he could feel the exchange of energy. Life for power, power for life. Fine. But it wouldn't be his. He growled and squeezed his writhing appendages together, and with a gasp of painful magical expenditure, dragged two of the girls back towards him.

As the two women, clad in nothing more than jewelry and thin silver chains, struggled against the unseen force that pulled them to their doom, Ibiranu surged to meet them. His right arm split apart, two of the tentacles wrapping around his weeping prey. He did not prolong their suffering, he was too hungry, too desperate. As soon as he wrapped the two women in his unnatural limb, he barked the words that would kill them and save his life.

He took everything from them, every drop of moisture, every ounce of vitality. The mouths in his arms bit them as he held them tight. Their screams became weaker with every passing second, until all that was left was terrified rasps, and then even that was done. He dropped them into the water. Two more corpses to feed his life, his vanity.

He looked down into the waters and was disgusted to see that the stolen life had done nothing for his twisted visage. He was still a monster, deformed and terrifying. A far cry from the beautiful man he once was. He twisted his right arm back together and looked back up at the door through which the women had fled. Even if he did not look like himself, he was back to his full strength. He had his magic, he even had his sword, still in its scabbard by his side.

The attack on the harem would bring guards; he would need to defend himself. Ibiranu moved through the door, striding with purpose now. He would not succumb to despair or violence. He would discover where he had been sent, and fight and kill his way back to Hemodiel's side to be healed of this deformation and kill the Sheyd who had done this to him.

After traversing a dim hall and ascending dimmer stairs, Ibiranu emerged in a massive temple hall. Marble walls and pillars, golden filigree, sconces with blazing torches, altars, and, of course, thrones. Thrones on which sat beings that reminded Ibi of Baal Hemodiel—gods. Ibiranu did not recognize the gods that sat on the raised thrones of gold-plated skulls and silver teeth. But they were unmistakable, from their eye-studded bodies, too-many arms, singed wings, and terrible cocks that would drag the floor if they rose. These were cut of the same cloth as his master.

The girls he had followed from the underground pools were crowded around the thrones, seeking protection from Ibiranu. The god on the right, a thick being of knotted muscle and bulging veins that wriggled under his red skin, stood and held out a hand. Ibiranu was lifted from the floor and floated forward. As powerless as the women had been against him, he was as impotent now. He was brought just before the god, who, with a twist of his hand, turned Ibiranu around slowly in the air as though examining him.

"I see you, little Phoenician." The god's voice was not the sibilant whisper of Baal Hemodiel but rather a crashing of stone against stone. "I see you have been touched by our kin and our enemies, sent by Hemodiel to my doorstep. Why?"

Ibiranu fell to the floor as the god released him from

his grasp. With a groan and a growl, he forced himself back to his feet, and then remembering himself, he fell to his knees, prostrate before the deity.

"Why do you kneel here now, before Refesh and Shadrap?" the god pressed.

Refesh, this was obvious now; who else could this mighty red-skinned god be but the lord of fire and lightning? Ibiranu glanced at the other god and noted the greenish skin, the slit eyes and scales that graced his skin; that could only be Shadrap.

"Mighty Refesh," Ibiranu began, returning his eyes to the floor before him, "I humbly beg your forgiveness for attacking your harem ..." In his mind, he was racing to remember what city the two gods would have been found in. Where had Baal Hemodiel sent him? He was about to continue his apology when he heard laughter from Refesh.

"Apologize for what? You hungered, you saw creatures weaker than you, and so you took what you wanted. Is this not the law? Do what you wilt, and if none can stop you, then it is within your rights. These slaves are food; their bodies, their wills, their lives, all of it exists for the pleasure of the mighty at the allowance of the strong."

Around Refesh, the women keened in fear. Had they fled to their master only to be given up to the monster that had appeared in their midst?

Ibiranu nodded slowly. He could feel the change within him, the mutating flesh barely kept in check by his will. "Carthage is under siege, attacked by—"

"By Ashmandai and his Sheydim. They are irksome

but of no more consequence than any insect. But you, who are you to bear the gifts of my brother and stand before me?"

Of no more consequence than insects? Ibiranu swallowed. Carthage burned, its populace facing slaughter at the hands of dragons and that terrible creature of darkness and shadow that had attacked him. Perhaps such creatures were beneath the notice of gods, but they were more than enough to destroy the mortal population of the city. Finally, he found his voice.

"I was defending Baal Hemodiel from an attack from a creature of darkness. The creature's power twisted me, changed me. To save me, my lord sent me … here." He still didn't know where "here" was. "I beg of you to heal me, undo the damage that your enemies have wrought so that I may continue to serve."

"That is what you were doing, slave of Hemodiel. Who. Are. You?" This time, Shadrap asked the question, his voice a thrumming disquiet thing, impossible to ignore or refuse.

"I am Ibiranu son of Hamilcar, heir of the royal family of Carthage, student of Baal Hemodiel, and the future warrior king!" He had said the words many times in the mirrors of his home. But the truth was that Carthage had not been ruled by a monarch in centuries; his nobility meant little other than being wealthy. His other mouths, the mouths along his arms and torso, laughed at his claim. They knew the truth and gibbered it out. *You are nothing, you are dirt, you are a toy, you are a boy built for the amusement of others.* But Baal Hemodiel had promised Ibi that with his magic tutelage, Ibi would be able to retake the throne from the corrupt Council of Elders and reign in power.

He could feel his stolen power waning, his arm writhing despite his effort to keep it still, his muscles wriggling under his flesh. He hungered. He kept his primary mouth shut, but the mouths that Ashmandai's twisted magic had caused murmured and whispered hateful threats in inhuman tongues towards the women. They cowered. Ibi tried to ignore the hunger.

"My gods, if you would grant me mercy, undo the horrid magic of your enemy, and return me to Baal Hemodiel's side, I will serve him once more and crush your enemies in the name of all the gods!" He practically begged them to make him whole. *We are you now, you are now whole,* his body promised him, giving a horrid voice to his fears. "I have long studied under his guidance. I have tremendous power … for a mortal—"

Refesh cut him off with a wave of his hand. "You are mortal, and your power is beneath us, Ibiranu son of Hamilcar. You are beneath …" He in turn was cut off by Shadrap, who whispered in his ear.

The god's whisper, indistinct, secretive, still thrummed through the temple, vibrating his bones, causing his creeping flesh to quiver as if in the throes of religious ecstasy. It was agony.

Refesh nodded, coming to some agreement with Shadrap. "But Ashmandai, insect that he is, is not beneath us, his magic a twisted reflection of the gods' power. We cannot undo what has been done to you."

21

Chapter Three

At the god's proclamation of his fate, three mouths tore open on Ibiranu's side and howled in anguish. The gnashing teeth tearing at his own ribs forced the prince to his knees, doubled over in pain. The rest of his mouths (how many were there?) screamed their terror.

Then he was silent.

He still screamed, he still hurt. But no sound escaped. He was so surprised to find himself silent that he almost didn't notice Refesh speaking to him, having used some godly magic to suck the sound out of the man.

"… not all is lost, princeling. There is a hope."

Slapping his tentacles against the floor, Ibi pushed himself up, trying to present himself as something other than the desperate and pathetic servant. "Hope?" he asked, hoping he didn't sound half as pitiful as he felt. His new mouths spoke too, repeating the word in fervent whispers.

"Hope." Refesh agreed. "Ashmandai's power is derived from the gods. Stolen from us centuries ago. He created a book, a tome wrapped in the flesh of our very children, inked in the blood of murdered divinity. *The Book of the Children*." The way it was intoned, the words had weight. They dragged the world into darkness with them. "A vile amalgamation of unholy knowledge in direct conflict with all things that are good in this world. As terrible as this book is, it will contain the knowledge necessary for us to heal your flesh, to make you whole again. There lies your hope, Ibiranu, student of Hemodiel, therein lies your quest."

Refesh pushed himself up, his towering form bulbous and grotesque. The eyes that covered the god stared at Ibi, vestigial arms wavering as if helping him balance. He took one ponderous step forward. His cock, a throbbing misshapen thing with tongues jutting from underneath the foreskin, twitched as it slid over the tiles, leaving a trail of bubbling semen behind. "A quest. You will fetch the book for us, prove your worth, prove your might. Bring the book to us, and you will ascend mortal limitations to sit at the right hand of the gods. Fail, and all that will be left of you will be the pain."

Ibiranu nodded, thankful to be given an opportunity not only for advancement but for growth, advancement into the pantheon of demigods. "I will do this. If I have to traverse the whole of the world and kill every demon, I will find your book."

"Then you are in luck, worm," Shadrap said. "You do not need to traverse the world and search the continents. Just one island. Et Adasi. The Isle of Flesh."

There were gasps from the other humans in the large

room, and for the first time, Ibiranu noticed that there were servants, attendants, priests, and guards in the temple with them. He had been so focused on his prey at first, and then his attention had been taken up by his gods. How had he missed all these others with all of his extra eyes? Now that he was aware, he also became aware of his panoramic vision. Almost every face in the room had blanched at the mention of this place. But Ibi had never heard of it.

"My lord, I am unfamiliar with this place, this Et Adasi, but I would travel to any land and conquer any foe to serve you." *To be healed.* "I will not be daunted in my service." *In my own ambition.* The voice that was normally just in his head, the truth, was now whispered by mouths he had no control over. He stood fast, though, standing by the lies he spoke with purpose.

The gods either didn't notice the chittering truth mumbled from his inhuman lips or chose to ignore it. What did they care of his intention or motives, so long as he served like the faithful dog he was. Shadrap reached out and plucked a woman off the floor. She struggled for a moment before the god whispered in her ear. Her ears bled at the sound, her eyes bulging, but she was calm. He set her down, and she loped away, bent over on all fours like an animal. Ibiranu watched her leave before his attention was brought back to Refesh speaking.

"We will see if you are capable; we will see our brother's training in action. As is the law, we may gift you three things, Ibiranu, prince of Carthage. Just three. The first we have given: the quest, the task, the opportunity for healing, and power beyond what you have imagined. And know, Ibiranu, that I know your heart. I know that your imagination has soared to the height of its limit with fantasies. But you should know that your fantasies are but the tip of the cock of possibility poised at the labia of true potentiality."

Ibiranu nodded, trying to hide his smile as his thoughts flared towards what could possibly be beyond what he had already spent countless hours meditating on. Several of his mouths drooled in hungry lust for the power that was promised.

"The second gift is more practical, more concrete, for even in the kingdom of gods, currency is required. I gift you this." The bloated god shifted his weight and kicked a loose pile of treasure, tribute paid to the god over the course of years. Gold coins, silver baubles, and precious gems clattered over the tile.

Ibiranu fell to his knees, scooping up the riches, his hands and tentacles wrapping around as much as he could carry. With this, he could buy a city, a country, an army of his own. It was more riches than all of Carthage had. Around him, the servants and adherents of Refesh fell to the floor to gather what had flown too far for Ibiranu to gather.

They fought for the wealth, blood spilling as guards drew swords and fanatics ripped flesh with teeth, all over a few coins. Within moments, the hall was a bloodbath as those loyal to the gods proved how little fraternity there was in their shared worship. Ibiranu watched through inhuman eyes, trying not to be drawn into the conflict; as he was beneath the gods, so this chafe was beneath him. If the gods ignored the jealous greedy squabble, then so would he.

"Take the wealth. Purchase the supplies and guides you will need from the marketplace of Rotachat," Refesh stated.

"And take this," Shadrap spat as the bestial harem girl returned, loping and frothing, driven mad by the commands of a god whispered in mortal ears. "This map will show the way to Et Adasi," Shadrap continued as the woman crawled forward and fell before Ibiranu, holding the map up to him in trembling hands.

Ibi took the map with his human hand, overwhelmed with the kindness the deities were showing him. Three gifts and the opportunity to grow in power and prestige. He did not deserve such reward, but neither would he turn it down. He studied the map so intently that, at first, he did not hear the woman's screams.

Without his conscious command, his tentacle arms had lashed out as he took her map, wrapping around the woman, constricting, each beaked and toothsome maw set in the suckers of his arm biting and tearing. Ripping her apart where she stood and devouring her flesh. Ibiranu pulled his tentacles back, horrified at what had happened. It was too late. The buxom woman fell dead, gaping holes torn in her flesh. Ibi looked up and realized that neither Refesh or Shadrap seemed perturbed by the girl's death. Their attention was instead on the chaos that filled the temple.

Ibi turned in a slow circle and saw the bloodbath that the loose riches had caused had now evolved. No longer were they killing each other. Now they were fucking. Robes and armor were shoved aside to allow access as those with the equipment strove to penetrate any orifice offered. They writhed and pummeled each other's sexes on top of the bleeding ruined corpses of those that had been killed seconds earlier. Some were still dying, their lasts breaths pushed out by the hammer-like desperation of those who still lived. Ibiranu gaped at the display of literal bloodlust. Those who had not found a living partner in the turmoil had turned to shoving their aching and engorged members into the corpse holes torn by spears and sword.

"Join them if you wish," Refesh cooed.

Ibi was horrified to find he wanted to. His cock ached, stiffened to full attention and leaking pre-ejaculate at the thought of taking his place in the bacchanal. But his skin writhed, it demanded change, it demanded that he accept the creeping corruption of his form. And that was unacceptable. He tore his eyes from the bodies of the men and women who were lost to the throes of some sick passion and bowed deeply to the gods.

"No, lords. I must go. I will find your book; I will undo Ashmandai's wicked mischief." Before he could be tempted by the offering of flesh, blood, and sex on display once more, Ibiranu ducked his head and fled the temple.

Pushing open the doors, he froze. He had known this was not the city of Carthage, but he was dumbfounded by the sight before him.

He did not recognize the land that stretched out before him at all. Not the city that seemed composed of metal and light below the temple, which sat on some high summit, nor the thick jungles that surrounded it. He did not know the shorelines or seas beyond. Even the waters of the ocean looked alien to him. They were not the rich blues of his home but rather turquoise and amethyst hues that seemed lit from beneath by some radiant light source. On the horizon he could see other land masses jutting from the strange ocean.

He stepped out of the temple, allowing the great door to close behind him, and pulled his robes tight, doing his best to conceal the monstrous nature of his right half. He held the map in his left hand, letting it unfurl. It was a nautical map, showing a great number of islands and landmasses set within the gem-colored seas. It was mostly written in a language Ibiranu could not read, one of snake-like lines, dots, and trembling symbols. But if Shadrap said it would assist, then Ibiranu would trust the map and honor the sacrifice of the woman he had killed. He tucked the map into his robe, jostling the treasure within.

Below him, the city gleamed in the light. The gods had commanded him to purchase supplies and guides in Rotachat. Ibi assumed it to be the name of the city below. With no other direction or purpose than following the dictates of his gods, he started down the side of the mountain.

Despite having seen the splendor of the strange city from above, Ibi was unprepared for how beautiful and how squalid it was close up. The buildings were crafted from stained glass and silver struts. Marble blocks threaded with silver and gold formed arches, pillars, and cornerstones. Even the lowliest hovel here in the city of gods was a testament to excess and eye blistering beauty. It was wealth and decadence beyond Ibiranu's wildest imagining. But at the same time …

The populace seemed destitute on the outskirts. Makeshift lean-tos stood almost so thick as to be a facade to the beautiful buildings. The homeless and penniless shuffled and skittered among the debris of their lives. They would not meet Ibi's gaze. He wondered if these were not slaves, so defeated and cowed as to be subservient to any who passed. From under his robes, he could hear his own whispering, begging him to sate his hunger on these dispossessed. Who would miss these?

He was on a mission from the very gods of his people, he was a prince, he had wealth. What were these? His hunger peaked, but he was no monstrous murderer to feed on other humans just to sate himself. But he had other, more reasonable, needs. He turned suddenly, ducking down an ally. Without even being aware of himself, he lashed out with his tentacles, his right arm peeling apart and separating into several tendrils that each whipped about, tearing a makeshift home apart, making short work of the fabrics stretched over a frame of garbage. Inside, an old man screamed in fear, cowering back.

Ibi opened all of the eyes on his head, the flesh peeling away from the angry orbs; each looked in a different direction. Every vagrant stood and stared, but none dared approach the stranger who had descended from the temple into their midst. None dared help the man. Some whispered about the "god-touched" or curses, but none approached. Ibiranu stepped over the mess he had made, stepping around the human filth and waste in the street to press the man into the glass wall of the building with his unaltered hand.

"The markets, slave, where are the markets?" Ibi hissed, his diction destroyed by the way his newly malformed mouth formed the words. The question was echoed all across Ibi's body. The man trembled in fear, his eyes wide with animal terror, sputtering as though unable to form words.

Ibiranu had no patience for the man. His hunger and the incessant voice of the alien cells in his body screamed at him to devour the man; he could feel saliva building up in his mouths. But he mentally recoiled from the thought. He was no cannibal; he was no monster. He reached up with his still-human hand and gripped the man's head in his palm. "You do not need to speak" he hissed, and intoned words of maleficent power.

He peeled the man's brain apart, physically and metaphorically. The scalp peeled back as though torn by taloned hands, the skull cracking and splitting apart, revealing the red of the meninges and blood brain barrier, then that ruptured, revealing the gray meat of the brain. This unraveled, pouring from his fractured skull and unfurling like a flower blooming, spilling his thoughts and memories out from the destroyed meat.

The man's eyes rolled back in his head, cranial fluid leaking from his nose, a low growling keen forming deep in the throat. But Ibiranu's attention was on the man's thoughts, invisible to human sight but all too visible to his magic and, unexpectedly, to the inhuman eyes that now dotted his right side. Still whispering horrid words of magic, hissed through his teeth, Ibiranu sifted through the memories of the man, pulling from him knowledge of the city. The man was painfully ignorant of the city, and of the gods that ruled it, but he knew where the market was. Or rather, he had known. Ibiranu devoured the knowledge and released the man.

He fell to the street, gray brains and blood sloshing from the hole in his head to mingle with the human feces and garbage that littered the street where these vermin lived. Within seconds, rat-like scavengers were already invading the man's head hole to tear at the meat within.

Ibiranu turned away from the scene, noting with pleasure how those who had been watching recoiled from him in fear. This was power, the power of gods. Back in Carthage, where he was known, he was respected for his wealth and the favor Baal Hemodiel had shown him but not honored for the power he himself held.

Here, now, they feared not his family, wealth, or station. They feared him, and it was intoxicating. But he was on a mission. Ibi glanced down at the vermin-violated corpse at his feet and turned to leave. No one stopped him, going so far as to turn their eyes down and avoid his many-eyed gaze, as if ashamed of their own weakness and cowardice. Unmolested, he made his way deeper into the city of Rotachat.

Chapter Four

Rotachat was unlike anything he had seen before, and yet there was comforting familiarity. The bustling streets, the sights, and the smells were the same as Carthage, the same as any large city located next to the ocean would be. But it was also as if he had stepped out of the world of men and into a city populated by legends and creatures from myth. Not all of them were myths that Ibiranu knew.

On the outskirts, he had only seen humans wasting in the gutters and filth. But here in the heart of Rotachat, all manner of creatures seemed to live and thrive unmolested. Indeed, they seemed to be a common sight. Ibiranu had closed his extra eyes, pulled his robes tight, even hiding the sword at his side to avoid stares, but now he doubted he would have even merited a second glance. All around him were human-animal hybrids, demons, creatures he had only heard described in the mad ramblings of drunkards, now on full display, not only there but going about business as though they were human. As though there was nothing extraordinary about them at all.

The world, this world, was so much more colorful than he was used to. He saw women with blue skin and hulking giants with scales and fins. Here was a creature that appeared to be half-spider with the torso of an ape. Everywhere he looked, there was something to force his mind to reel from the sheer strangeness of this new world.

Was this place, this city, where all legends came from? And why? Why would the gods allow the Sheydim and demon-kind in their city? The only explanation Ibi could think of was that these were creatures who had surrendered, who had bowed to the gods in supplication. But if that were the case, why did they live and thrive in the city center while humans, god-created humans, lived in such destitute conditions on the outer edge? These questions and more filled Ibiranu's mind, but his first priority was to find passage to Et Adasi, retrieve the book, and be healed by the gods.

Being on a mission from the gods filled Ibi with pride. Sure, he had studied under Baal Hemodiel. Learned magic and war from a god. But being given a task, a quest, that was something else entirely. This was him being useful, not a favored toy but a hero in and of his own right. He was a player on the stage of the gods, and he would not fail.

Without too much issue, he was able to find the docks. He followed the fish folk. Those hulking men with scales and fins, with eyes too large and wide for their heads, grew more and more numerous the closer he came to the coast. He saw people, if they could be called people, with barnacles growing on their flesh who seemed to be as much anemone as people. He saw women with crusted shells and massive pincers. And the smell of salt water and rotting wood grew ever stronger as he followed the sound of shipyard bells and strange aquatic humanoids.

The ships of Rotachat were just as varied and strange as the population.

There were ships that seemed alive, wooden planks embedded in the backs of strange cephalopods and crustacean sea creatures whose giant eyes rolled madly in their alien skulls. The behemoths were lashed by chains to the docks. Despite their obvious discomfort, they stayed still and did not buck against the restraints as crewmen and shipwrights worked on building upon these living vessels.

There were ships that were more mundane, wood and iron lashed together in what he recognized from his own home. But even these bore weapons and flew flags that seemed impossible and inhuman, had mast configurations that hung and jutted at impossible angles that hurt his eyes to look on.

He saw ships made of gemstones and gold and marble, things that could not possibly stay afloat, carved with arcane runes that allowed the gaudy flotilla to stay above the gentle waves of the shipyard. These piers were patrolled by hulking things in the armor of the temple guard. These, then, were the ships of the gods.

For a moment, Ibiranu considered walking up to the guarded pier and demanding passage; he was royalty, but not only that, he was a servant of Baal Hemodiel, on a quest for Refesh! But no, the gods had gifted him with a veritable kingdom's worth of wealth to pay for passage and crew. While it would feel legendary to ride the strange glowing sea on the magic ships of gods, he understood somewhere deep inside his mutating and quivering flesh that this was as much a test as a quest. Relying on the power of others would not do. He turned from the impossible vessels and scanned the piers for a ship worthy of carrying him, worthy of his task.

Try as he might, though, he was not a seaman. While others his age had served in the naval forces aboard ships, Ibiranu had spent those years in the study of the occult. He could fight with a sword or a spear but had no eye or knowledge for the ships before him. But one thing that Ibi did understand was bureaucracy. He turned his eyes from the ships to the people. They scuttled and scurried, loading cargo, working thick ropes, and generally going about their lives. After a few moments, Ibi found what he was looking for; the obvious duties and duress of the harbormaster.

The man, towering and gray, with solid black eyes and the terrible teeth of a shark, was barking orders, lumbering around the docks on one peg leg as he oversaw the chaos. At the moment, he was berating three ship hands who seemed to be sheepishly arguing port feeds with him. Ibi waited for a moment, respectful of the man's duty and his standing, until the surly and shark-like man had finished dealing with the three. As they walked away, Ibi was quick to approach before a new responsibility should rear its head.

"Pardon, harbormaster," he said, the mouths hidden by his robe echoing his words in singsong whispers.

The shark-man looked down at him. Now standing next to him, Ibi saw that the harbormaster was a towering creature, easily three or four heads taller than him and packed with muscle.

The man's lipless mouth opened to bare his terrifying teeth in a bit of a snarl, though Ibiranu was unsure if the gesture was intended to intimidate him or was actually a signal of irritation. "What, scum?"

Ibi bristled at being called scum but had to remind himself that his station, wealth, and mission would mean very little if the monstrous man before him tore his throat out with his teeth.

"I am on a …" Ibi paused, not sure he wanted to advertise the full scope of his mission. "I am looking for a ship to commission. To take me to Et Adasi. The best available. I was—"

He was cut off as the harbormaster raised one huge hand to wave his words away, already bellowing a cruel laughter. "Et Adasi? Little human, no one sails for Et Adasi! If you seek death, there are easier ways, cleaner ways to achieve this."

Ibiranu frowned at the statement but shook his head. "I assure you, I have no intention of dying, and I have plenty of coin to pay for the best." He reached into his robe with his human arm and pulled out a large gemstone. "And to pay the person who points me in the right direction."

The man's broad head tilted, his black eyes locking onto the glittering prize in Ibi's hand. Something akin to laughter rumbled deep in his throat as he reached for the stone. But Ibi snatched it back before the man could take it. Let greed do the talking, Ibi thought, it always made things so much easier.

The harbormaster looked like he would simply tear Ibi's head off and take the stone for a moment, but instead, he stroked his chin and shrugged. "It is your funeral, human. The best will not go, but perhaps the adventurous will." He turned his head and smiled, his mouth opening to reveal those horrendous teeth as he laughed at some joke Ibi wasn't privy to. "Or the desperate. Captain Oshaank may accept your offer, but I would hurry if I were to want to hire the captain or their ship."

"Where can I find him?" Ibi asked, tired of the back-and-forth games and idle threats. The sooner he found this captain, the sooner he could be on his way and one step closer to returning to his normal human form. The squirming under his flesh was not subsiding, not getting any easier to ignore.

"They'll be at a bar, likely Azazel's Goat. But again, human, I would hurry. You are not the only one looking for them, just the only one looking that is not seeking to rectify a debt." The harbormaster held out his hand expectantly for payment.

Ibi held out the gem, but did not release it into the

waiting hand. "Point me in the right direction; where is this goat bar?"

The shark-like man grabbed the gem, wrenching it from Ibiranu's grasp, and grinned, turning it in his hand. Without looking away from the stone, he gestured to the side. "Just beyond the docks, you'll find 'em. Can't guarantee you'll find 'em in one piece."

Ibiranu nodded and hurried in the direction the harbormaster pointed, leaving him to appreciate his new wealth for just a moment before the chaos of the docks crashed back in on him. Ibi was not worried; if there was only one ship and captain that would be willing to travel to Et Adasi, surely then it was the most capable and the most fearsome captain in this strange land. With these thoughts stealing his heart, Ibiranu made his way through the street traffic and pushed open the doors of Azazel's Goat.

Inside was chaos. Ibi was not a complete stranger to such scenes; he had watched as soldiers celebrated the night before war, with emotions high and bravado masking fear. Half-dressed women and men of various species lounged in the laps of scarred and burly men, while in other parts of the tavern, sailors and soldiers wagered, played games of chance, told tales, and sang songs. It was a cacophonous wall of sound. The smell of saltwater and alcohol was so thick within the tavern that Ibi felt he had to push through it as a physical force.

Steeling himself against the chaos, Ibiranu forced his

way through the crowd. He was a strong man, used to exertion and battle, but these were naval warriors and sailors whose every day and waking moment was dedicated to physical labor, who lived and died by the strength of their arms in a storm. They dwarfed the mutated sorcerer. Ibi pushed past one man, who seemed more cuttlefish than man, cursing under his breath about the mucusy slime the contact left on his robes.

Not quietly enough.

The man-cuttlefish turned and glared at Ibi, his face, pale and marred by flailing tendrils surrounding a beakish mouth, twisted into a hateful scowl. "What did you say, human?" he asked, reaching for Ibi.

Ibi took several steps back until someone behind him shoved him forward, back into the cuttle-man. He balked, trying to figure out some way to diffuse the situation.

"Asked you a fuckin' question, dry-skin. What. Did. You. Say." It wasn't a question, it was a threat, or more accurately, it was the promise of an orgy of violence against Ibiranu's flesh.

He was about to answer when he heard something across the bar.

"No more time, Oshaank, no more excuses. Now we carve what's due from your hide."

Ibi peeked around the shoulder of the cuttle-man and saw a group of sailors closing in on a woman who was as much crab as she was person. She was thick, with hard shell covering much of her arms, one ending in a massive claw. On eye was human, blue and baleful, glaring out with hate. The other was a black orb topping a stalk of flesh. This was Oshaank? Ibi made to step around the cuttle-man, the confrontation forgotten as he saw the captain, when his aggressor shoved him back.

"Talking to you, dry-skin. You got a fuckin' problem with your fuckin' ears?"

Ibi turned his eyes back to the cuttle-man. He didn't want to start a fight, not here, surrounded by surely sailors. He recognized that it would only take a spark to light this whole establishment into violence. But if he didn't act quickly, then the debt-collectors would kill his only hope for reaching Et Adasi. He had no choice.

"What I said," Ibi began, drawing himself up, trying to look as intimidating as possible, "is that your slime has marred my robes, and I am too busy to deal with you or your slime right now." He allowed his misshapen tentacles to fall from his robe. They writhed at the promise of violence. He could feel the smaller cilia on his face unfurling, pulsing. His extra mouths opened and spat curses, mocking the cuttle-man.

"Is this supposed to impress me, Cursed-One? You fell out of favor with the gods, and now you think you will find favor here?" The cuttle-man reached forward, but Ibi had been prepared. He stepped forward inside the man's reach and placed a hand on the man's chest. With a few whispered words, he froze the air and that flesh within the air around his hand.

The man screamed, falling backward as the ice ate into his flesh, spreading from where Ibi had touched him. His heart seized and shredded itself apart as it pumped crystallized frozen blood through delicate veins. Within seconds, blue blood was spluttering from his mouth and nose. His fall had been enough to knock another man to the floor, who in turn lifted and swung a chair at Ibiranu.

The impact flung him against a table, spilling drinks everywhere, which is when the brawl truly took a life of its own. The cuttle-man survived long enough to be trampled to death as his frozen blood eviscerated him from the inside out.

The brawl was not an ideal situation. Ibi now had to contend with violence from every angle, but at least it was no longer focused on him. Likewise, the distraction of the fight seemed to have given Oshaank an edge against her aggressors. She had hopped the bar and now held a wickedly curved blade up, keeping the men back. Ibi worked his way towards her, determined to extricate the captain and his mission from the situation.

Reaching her, he wrapped his human hand around her upper arm, surprised to find soft skin there, meeting the crustacean armor of her forearm. "Captain Oshaank?" he asked, then continued when she gave a short nod. "My name is Ibiranu, come with me," he hissed.

Jerking her arm away, the large woman growled, revealing a mouth filled with mandibles and crushing plates. "Why should I?" she asked as she ducked under a thrown stool and swung at a man passing by.

"Because eventually this brawl will end and your debtors will come to kill you. Come with me and earn money, or stay and die skewered on their swords."

She looked like she wanted to argue, but an offering of money was a siren call she could not resist. She cast one last look around the bar before nodding. She grabbed Ibi's arm and dragged him through the throng of battling sailors. Each step was plagued by stray punches and airborne objects, curses, spells, swords, daggers. Despite their hasty retreat, it seemed more of a battle to leave the fight than to stay in it. But within minutes, Oshaank had dragged him out of a side door and into the ally.

They spent a few moments catching their breath while listening to the din just inside, Ibi sitting on a nearby crate and Oshaank leaning against the wall. Despite it all, the danger, violence, and chaos, she wore a huge smile. Ibi could see that she lived for this, she was a thrill-seeker, the most short-lived and dangerous sort of person to be around. But the most likely to become involved in suicidal missions. That's why the harbormaster had singled her out.

"Now ..." Oshaank broke the moment of rest. "Speak, human; you said you had coin. Where are we sailing?"

43

Chapter Five

"Et Adasi?" Oshaank sputtered. "Are you insane? There are easier ways to die."

Ibiranu rolled his eyes and shook his head. "You and everyone seem to think that it's a death sentence, but—"

"Because it is, dry-skin!" Oshaank interrupted him. "Worse, than! Everyone who has made that trek, that voyage—"

"Doesn't come back, I get it," Ibi said, exasperated.

"No! They do. There are things worse than death, and Et Adasi is their origin. Why the fuck would you want to travel to that gods-forsaken place? Why would you risk it? Ask me to risk it?"

"Because I have been commanded by the gods!" Ibiranu snapped. Eyes peeled open on his head, causing Oshaank to recoil from him. "I go because it is how I regain my humanity, how I attain power beyond what small-minded fools can dream of, and you ..." He paused, his voice dripping with venom. "You go because I can pay you more wealth than you can ever spend. I can give you so much that no one ever says you have debt so long as you live. But if it pleases you, I'll just buy your ship and find sailors who aren't cowards to take me on my journey."

Her human eye narrowed at being called a coward. She spoke in a quiet hiss. "I have been called many things, you God-Cursed piece of shit. But not a coward, not a fucking coward."

"Perhaps it is a new appellation for you, but it is one that is fitting, unless you care to prove me wrong, prove everyone wrong. Imagine, the wealth yes, but also the legend, being the only …" he paused. She wasn't really a person, or a human … what was she? What were the sea-folk? "Sailor … to voyage to Et Adasi and come back, not only in one piece but triumphant as well." His mouths spat the insult: *coward, coward, coward, coward, coward.*

"Even if I wanted to die, even if I wanted my soul torn to shreds, there are no reliable lanes to traverse, no currents to carry us to Et Adasi. Its location isn't known, not by entities that will share it," Oshaank said. "It is not cowardice to be practical."

Ibiranu reached into his robes and pulled out the map the gods had given him. "This? This is your mighty hurdle? This is your excuse?" He unfurled it and watched as Oshaank's eye widened. She understood what she was looking at, she understood what it meant.

Oshaank hissed through the plates of bone that could be called teeth in a human. He could see her will to survive was battling with her will to go where others wouldn't. After a moment, she nodded. "It will cost you, God-Cursed …"

"You say cursed, but they have gifted me with a kingdom of riches to pay for this quest. A kingdom I will share with you, and your crew." Ibiranu responded, already turning away. He knew she was convinced. All that remained was negotiating a price, and he didn't care about the wealth he had now; it would be nothing compared to the wealth he would have at the culmination of this quest. "I hope your ship is at least worth the price and hassle of attaining your services?"

"Ah, about my ship …" Oshaank said, an odd quality to her voice.

"You do have a ship," Ibiranu said. It wasn't a question, she had to have a ship. Why would she be a captain if she didn't have a ship?

"Well, no, I don't own a ship; ship owners generally hire captains, until they can hire their own crews to man their ships," she explained.

Ibiranu turned, glaring at the woman, "So you are saying I need to buy a ship and hire a crew?" *A waste of time, a waste of flesh, flense her, eat her, be done with her.*

She raised her hands in self-defense. "Listen, it isn't an issue. Do you want a good ship, or do you want a ship that money can buy?"

"I already said money isn't an issue." Ibiranu snarled, exhausted by the roundabout guessing game the captain was making him play. *It is the only issue, the only currency worth the time of mortals.* His mouths echoed.

"And I say that money isn't what you need. First, we get the crew, then we procure a ship."

"Procure," Ibiranu repeated. His eyes, all of them, narrowed in suspicion.

"Yes, procure, the best ships aren't for sale, aren't for hire. And to make it to Et Adasi, more importantly, to make it back, we need a ship that can out-sail all but the most robust of best of her majesty's navy."

Ibiranu was about to ask about who her majesty was; who would be queen in a land ruled by gods? But Oshaank was already pushing past him and heading towards another end of the docks.

"Come on, dry-skin," She called over her shoulder. "We'll need to flash your money wisely in order to get the best sailors for the job, but don't you worry you're cursed flesh about it, I know exactly who to bring."

Who to bring, it turned out, was another fishman. Ibiranu wondered, in the back of his mind, if the creature standing in front of him would be offended by being called a fishman. This one looked more akin to a prawn—short, pale pink skin, with small vestigial arms jutting from his chest that wrung themselves nervously as he spoke to Oshaank. They spoke in some strange flowing language that rolled off their tongues, only to be punctuated by clicks, squeals, and growls. Ibiranu disliked not being able to understand them as they spoke, suspicious they would make plans to drag him into a back alley and kill him for his wealth.

He watched their body language carefully. He knew that viziers, ambassadors, and spies were masters of the art of weaseling out and telling lies. He had no training in detecting deception, nor was he familiar with how creatures such as these, with their extra arms and eye stalks, would manifest their duplicity. Ibi flexed his hand, worrying at his fingers as he waited for one of them to speak in a language he could understand.

After what felt like too long a time, Oshaank broke from the shrimp-man-thing and turned back to Ibiranu, nodding.

"Okay, we have our crew," she said.

"Him? He is our crew?" *Crew? He is food, they are all food, all of them,* the mouths echoed, but now he was almost sure that only he could understand their sibilant whispers.

"No, that *Pensi* is just a negotiator for the rest of his crew, but his crew is fearless and complete, so we don't need to draft or to press gang anyone in; we can just do what comes naturally."

"Which is to steal a ship, board it with ... shrimp-men, and set sail?" Ibiranu asked, skeptical of the diminutive, nervous-looking man she had been speaking to.

"Not so loud!" Oshaank hissed, looking around the crowded bar nervously. "Are you daft, dry-skin? Stealing a ship is our best option for a good ship, that doesn't mean we won't all be hung for doing so. Keep your fucking mouths shut until we are safely on board. Then you can ask all your questions."

Ibiranu was about to reprimand her for thinking she could speak to him that way, but she was already turning and leaving. Left sputtering, Ibiranu had no choice but to follow in her wake.

He found her a second later on the street. She glanced over her shoulder at him and nodded towards the docks. She was appraising the ships like a woman at the market, looking over each vessel as if they were fish on display and she was deciding which would be the tastiest for dinner. Ibiranu looked out over the ships, trying to see what she was seeing, but it was too dark for him to really make out much, the streetlamps doing little to illuminate the ships. Even if he could see, he wasn't sure he would know what he was looking at.

"There," she finally said, nodding towards the north end of the docks. "There's our ship." She turned and walked down the street, not approaching the ships but heading in the direction she had indicated.

Ibiranu stared where she had pointed, trying to discern what differentiated that ship from the dozen or so others. "What makes that ship different than any of these others? What makes a ship swifter?" he asked.

She scowled over her shoulder at him. "I imagine you would have stolen a human boat, one with the gilded edges, maybe even one from the gods," Oshaank said. She laughed when Ibi didn't respond. "Of course you would have, dry-skin, your kind always believe you are superior to Siren, even when it comes to nautical prowess. Imagine. Imagine thinking you are better at mastering the sea than those that come from it. Humans' hubris knows no bounds. The ship we are taking is a Siren ship, built for speed and maneuverability. The seas, especially the routes I saw on your little map, are teeming with beasts and danger, things that you would be better to outrun than face. For that, we need a ship that understands and rides the ocean, not one that plows through it with human arrogance and incompetence."

Again, Ibiranu wanted nothing more than to confront the woman on her insulting derision towards human kind, but what would he say? He didn't know anything about ships or sailing, and he knew even less about the so-called Siren. He knew there were legends of Siren, half-bird women who sang songs promising knowledge that drove men mad. But he had the feeling she was speaking of the fish-men he had seen all over the docks, like herself.

But now he didn't have time to think about the alien world he found himself in nor the nature of his companion. Already he could see the small shadows of the diminutive shrimp-men that Oshaank had called Pensi moving across the street and approaching the shipyard.

"I hope you are not opposed to blood, dry-skin," Oshaank whispered as she slunk forward, drawing a barnacle crusted sword as she moved.

Ibiranu watched her, frowning. He didn't understand why this subterfuge was necessary. She claimed that the ship wouldn't be for sale, but perhaps she didn't understand the sheer amount of wealth he had been given by the gods, a wealth that had driven their own guards and courtesans to madness and murder. But on that same note, he was not opposed to bloodshed. He was a warrior and a killer. And now, something maybe worse.

Though his human tongue had not tasted her, he had devoured that servant girl in the temple. He knew the taste of her meat and flesh, and he found it calling to him. He could devour them whole, steal their essence while at the same time tearing their meat off of their bones. And he wanted to; he wanted to find more pitiful humans and make a meal of them. In some part of his mind, he recoiled from the monstrous thought, but in another, he accepted it. Was he not a prince? Lesser humans were just that, lesser, upon this earth to serve him and to be served to him.

Steeling his resolve, he hurried to join Oshaank—after all, what harm was stealing a ship when it should have been his by right? Hunger gnawed at his thoughts, and a greasy power gathered at his fingertips. It was his magic, but it was more, sentient and eager to tear reality apart.

Chapter Six

By the time Oshaank and Ibiranu reached the ship, the attack was already underway. The Pensi, slight as they might be, moved quickly, wielding strange curved daggers that plunged into the crew who were aboard. The first part of whatever plan Oshaank and the Pensi had concocted seemed to be going off perfectly, and Ibiranu was almost irritated that he had missed the chance to bring his own power to bear, to show his new crew and their victims his might.

He was about to push his hunger down when a roar shook the ship. The shape of a Pensi, broken, cracked, and bleeding, hurled past him. Ibiranu looked in the direction the dead sailor came from and spotted the massive shape of a man swinging a cannon around as easily as some might wield a mace. Behind him, more massive shapes were emerging from the hold. These, Ibiranu assumed, were the guards, set here to protect this ship.

The Pensi were fleeing the huge shapes, but Oshaank had set her jaw and was stalking forward, ready to fight; perhaps her crablike shell was better armor than whatever the more diminutive beings had. Ibi was about to ask Oshaank for her plan when one of the giants charged forward with a roar. There was no time to think, only react.

Ibi dove over the side of the ship, his tentacle arm lashing out to grab at the railing, catching him and allowing him to swing back up onto the side. But now instead of being before a charging elephant of a man, he was behind him. Ibiranu lifted his hand and gestured at the man, building his willpower into a tangible force. He chanted a loud curse, even as the man turned to bring his cannon back around to aim at Ibi, each of his mouths echoing the curse, manipulating it, magnifying it.

The mouth of the cannon lined up with Ibiranu's head, but before the man could fire, his arm went limp, dropping the artillery. His screams came next. Ibiranu smiled. He was growing fond of the sound of screams; the way they echoed and warped in aura of his power was a music unlike any other in this world. The man opened his mouth, his eyes wide with fear, and a bloody, skeletal hand, his hand, ripped out of his mouth and groped for leverage.

Ibi was so focused on forcing the man's bones to pull themselves from his soon-to-be corpse that he did not see the battle Oshaank was fighting against one of the other men, nor the third man coming up behind him. Both of his victim's bony arms protruded from his mouth now, choking off his screams as they pushed at his face to pull further out, his fleshy limbs limp and powerless at his side. But before he could enjoy any more of the spectacle, the third sailor swung an anchor at him.

He caught it in his tentacles without even being aware that's what he was doing. Still, the impact flung him, and he would have been battered across the ship if his biting cephalopodic arm hadn't held on. Instead, he swung around and landed on the back of the third sailor. Ibiranu gritted his teeth, his eyes glowing black holes of terrible unholy light as he forced the power of earthly creation through the back of the sailor's skull.

Within seconds, stinging insects began to pour out of the man's eye sockets, nose, and mouth, his entire cranium filling with an unending spring of the crawling horror. Ibi could see through the man's flesh and bone, see the biting skittering things tearing at his brain meat, burrowing through the pink and red folds, devouring him from the inside out. Ibi's eyes dimmed, his vision returning to normal as he looked around at the carnage surrounding him.

Before the invasion of Carthage yesterday, though it seemed like centuries ago, Ibiranu had never seen such visceral violence and bloodshed. Now, it seemed as though it followed him. The war, the throne room of Refesh, and now this ship, all sites of intense and bloody combat, all charnel houses marking his deeds. He did not lament this fact; he was unbothered. In truth, this bothered him more than the deeds, that he should be inured to the violence and savagery with which he acted. He had always believed other men to be beneath him, but now they seemed less like men and more like beasts worthy of nothing but butchery.

He peered down at the half-human corpse at his feet. It still writhed with the insects that Ibiranu had crafted from the void. It was a strange merging of flesh and carapace, a human in some ways, but in so many more, a creature of the sea. Perhaps that was why he felt nothing, because they were nothing. They were not his equal beings; they were to be used and discarded, or simply obliterated if they got in his way.

The sound of screaming brought him back to the present. Oshaank was jamming her massive crab claw into the eye socket of the man she had been fighting. Her human eye lit with an intense and feverish light as she forced the too-large appendage in. The skull cracked and split apart, the jelly of ocular fluid and brain tissue squishing out from around her pincer as she tore the man's head apart. It was a gruesome sight but no more so than what he had himself done.

The ship was quiet but for the mewling of the not yet dead who littered the deck. The Pensi were making quick work of them, though, several of them grabbing the bodies of the dead and dying and dragging them underneath.

"What are they doing?" Ibi asked as he approached the panting form of Oshaank. "Wouldn't it be better to dump them over the side?" He twisted out of the way as one of the shrimp-folk rushed past him on some task of setting the ship free to sail.

"No, on many counts, God-Cursed. The blood in the water would no doubt draw more Siren, more dangerous Siren at that. Besides, I didn't see you carrying a lot of goods and stock for the voyage; we'll need to eat something." She turned and began walking towards the bow of the ship.

The casual suggestion of cannibalism ought to have turned his stomach, but again, Ibiranu was having trouble seeing the dead humanoids as men; no, they were things. And why should it bother him to devour the flesh of things? *It shouldn't. They were weaker, they died, and therefore you own them, we own them, the stronger devours the weaker, the universe is devoured by its masters, you are the master.*

Ibiranu shook the words whispered by the mouths dotting his body out of his head before following after Oshaank to the front of the ship.

Before long, they were out to sea, the diminutive Pensi scurrying about their duties faster than any human crew that Ibiranu had witnessed back in Carthage. Ibi watched as the lights of Rotachat grew smaller and smaller on the horizon, eventually disappearing altogether. Having never been to sea, he was in awe at the great expanse of water and sky; the agoraphobic immenseness of the world around them would be crippling if not for the beauty of it.

He stood there on the portside deck for a long time, listening to the waves slap against the ship, a hypnotic and soothing sound that drowned out the constant chittering and demands of his new body, if just for a moment. It was disturbing how strange this place was, and the young prince had to wonder if he had been killed and was now experiencing some horrible afterlife. Did the dead know they were such? But if he were alive and this was no nightmare, then—he looked down at his mutated form, his ruined body—could fetching the gods' book restore him to his natural form? Could it return him home? If not, he would need to make the best of this new world he found himself in.

Ibiranu turned and crossed the deck towards the helm, where Oshaank stood surveying the stars. She moved from an astrolabe to the map, somehow coordinating the two tools and the ship to drive them towards their destination, a magic that Ibiranu could never understand.

"You said that there were more dangerous Siren in the waters surrounding Rotachat," he said without preamble. "What are Siren, exactly?" *Bastard leftovers from the chaos,* his other mouths answered in their terrible, gibbering language.

Oshaank turned her eye stalk towards him before shaking her head and rolling up the map. "You're not from the islands, are you? You're from somewhere beyond the mists. Out in the gray."

Ibiranu bristled at the condescending way she spoke, that incessant voice in his ear urging him to rip her apart. But he didn't even understand what she was saying, what she was asking. "What do you mean by beyond the mists and out in the gray?"

Oshaank let out a little huff, a laugh at his ignorance. "Where we are, this ocean, the islands, it's surrounded on all sides by a thick mist. Sometimes people or things come through it, will of the gods, I suppose; but on the other side, there's another world, a larger, bigger world. That's what I've heard anyway. No one but the gods can escape this place, not really."

Not dead then, but a different world, a different reality? The question then was no longer where Baal Hemodiel had sent him but why Baal Hemodiel had sent him here. He was going to press for more information on the so-called islands when Oshaank interrupted his train of thought by answering his first question.

"I guess you don't have Siren in your world, or whatever part of your world you come from. But the Siren are the sea-folk. We come from the ocean, from the mighty kingdom of Ahtaea that rests beneath the waves in the deepest reaches of this cursed sea."

"So, all of you ... fish-folk are Siren?" Ibiranu asked. He had already seen a dazzling array of humanoid sea-creatures.

"Fish-folk? Do I look like a fucking fish?" she snapped. Ibiranu stuttered, taken aback by the sudden venom in her voice. A moment later, she burst into laughter. "Watch who you use that term with; some Siren would eat your lungs for using the phrase. But yes, the Siren are the people of the sea." She paused to lean over the railing of the ship, staring into the waters as if she could see to the bottom of the ocean. "Ahtaea is a wonderous place, God-Cursed. Beautiful beyond compare."

"So why come to the surface? If it's so wonderful, I've seen so many fi—" He stopped himself. "Siren in Rotachat, your underwater city must be empty."

"Althaea is no city, it is an empire," Oshaank corrected, a hint of despair in her voice. "And those you see on the surface are refugees, exiles, immigrants; we come to the surface to escape."

"Escape what?" Ibiranu asked.

"Slavery, servitude, oppression. On the surface, you serve your gods, everyone serves them, even those who they cursed. But beyond that, you are your own woman. Your life is your own." She waved a claw at Ibiranu's writhing right arm. "But down there, we live in a caste system based on our species, and it is cruel. First you must serve our absentee gods, and then their priests. The Selur rule the kingdom beneath the priests, then the Kaldeni, then the Jelani, and so on and so forth, all the way down to the Pensi, who are viewed as little more than useful foodstuffs. Cruelty is only curbed when dealing with your equals or betters. Towards someone of … lower birth …" she nearly spat the word. "Towards someone of lower birth, there is no reason to be kind, no reason to show mercy, or love." She shook her head, her entire carapace trembling with barely contained hatred.

"Those Siren you see in Rotachat or anywhere on the surface are escaping a life of painful servitude or have been forced out of our homes due to the political games of higher-born nobles."

Oshaank fell silent, and Ibiranu did not know what to say. He understood the terms; he himself was a noble, he had treated serfs and servants like chattel for his amusement. But pointing out that nobility and serfdom were a natural part of the order of society would likely cost him his crew, and possibly his life. He turned his eyes, all of his eyes, instead to the place where the stars met the sea on the horizon.

There was a scuttling across the deck. The two turned to watch as a Pensi, perhaps the same one Oshaank had been dealing with in town, approached. It spoke quickly, clearly agitated, in that flowing, clicking language before stepping back. Oshaank's eyes went wide.

"What? What is it?" Ibi demanded.

"They found something below deck ..." Oshaank whispered, clearly excited by the news.

"What? What did they find?" *Food. Food for tearing and sapping the vitality out of!*

Oshaank turned to him, her lips peeling back in a wide smile revealing an unfurling proboscis that ran across her teeth-plates. "A prisoner."

Chapter Seven

It was indeed a prisoner. Hidden in the shadows cast by the lantern sputtering just outside the brig was a figure clothed in chains and rags. It was difficult to make out, but its eyes were glowing in the gloom, bleeding a painful violet light into the room. Whatever the prisoner was, it wasn't human. Ibiranu stood just outside of the barred door, staring in, his left hand on his hip, his right tentacle-arm undulating calmly. He was getting better at controlling it. Oshaank and the Pensi stood on either side of him.

Oshaank cleared her throat. "What should we do with it?"

"Figure out what it is first, and why it's locked up second, I would imagine." Ibiranu answered. A prisoner on a Siren ship, Ibiranu had no idea what that could mean. Were the surface Siren at war with anyone? Had the prisoner done something unspeakable? Perhaps it was one of the Ahtaean nobles Oshaank had shown such hatred for.

"Figuring it out should be simple enough," Oshaank admitted, turning and barking some order at the Pensi.

The prawn-man balked and scurried away, returning seconds later with another Pensi. Ibiranu was having difficulty telling them apart. They seemed to be bickering in their strange language.

"What is happening?" Ibi asked Oshaank.

"They are trying to argue about which one of them should go into the cell and goad our … guest into the light," she answered.

It was a death sentence; Ibiranu knew that, so did the two Pensi. On one hand, Ibiranu didn't care enough to find out who the prisoner was; what did it matter? After all, the presence of the prisoner, regardless of its identity, would not change their goal. He had to reach Et Adasi, he had to retrieve the book, and he had to return home to Baal Hemodiel. On the other tentacle, Ibi was irritated by the creatures' cowardice.

Almost without thinking, Ibi grabbed the door to the cell and pulled it open. His tentacle lashed out, wrapped around one of the arguing Pensi, and threw them into the cell before slamming the door shut once more. The Pensi pulled itself up and took two steps towards the door before the prisoner shifted. The shadows in the room grew longer, seeming to writhe as they surrounded the prawn-man. The figure with the glowing eyes emerged from the darkness, grabbing the back of the Pensi's head and dragging him back to the wall of the cell.

The three of them watched as the prisoner began to ram the Pensi's head into the wall. Each impact became wetter. The first few had been hard cracks against the Pensi's shell, but by the fourth hit, the meat of the Pensi was exposed, sliced apart by its own shell and the wood. Blood splattered against Ibiranu as the creature was brutally murdered. But even when the Pensi stopped struggling, the prisoner was not done.

It charged forward into the light, the Siren's body held in front of it. With a ringing sound, the prisoner forced the Pensi's body against the cell and then began crushing and forcing the broken form through the bars. Ibiranu watched passively, keeping his face blank, though he was secretly horrified by the brutality he was witnessing. Was it any different than what he and Oshaank had done on the deck? Seeing another enact the same ferocious cruelty he was capable of was sobering, but he was resolute that none here would see him tremble.

The gore was incredible. Blood and guts washed at his feet, but Ibi instead focused on the prisoner themself. The figure was dressed in rags, its face twisted in hateful violence. But it was beautiful. Almost breathtakingly so. An androgyny that was completely alluring, neither feminine nor masculine but somehow both at once. Perfect porcelain skin that seemed to shift from pale to dark as the shadows played against it. Waves of black hair fell around its face, tangled with blood and shell from its kill. Its violet eyes seemed to glow brighter as it killed, and its full, inviting lips were pulled back in a snarl.

Ibiranu was captivated, noticing the long, tapered ears, the way its fingers ended in talons rather than nails. But then he noticed that across its body were tattoos that glowed gently, and his heart sank. He knew what this alluring creature was; he understood now what they had locked in their brig, though he couldn't fathom how they kept it so. He had hoped, in fact, that none of these creatures had made it through the veil and he would be free of their horrid existence until he returned triumphant.

"Gods," Oshaank murmured as the last bits of the Pensi were forced through the bars.

"Hardly," Ibiranu growled, moving as close as he dared to the barred door. "I know what you are, creature, I know what you are capable of, and I know you can be killed." *Then kill it!* Ibi's eyes narrowed as he watched the beautiful creature stalk back into the shadows at the back of the cell. Such violence, such beauty, Ibi almost didn't notice one of his tentacles slowly stroking his erection. He pulled his arm away from himself, disturbed by his own arousal. "No ... no god."

Ibiranu turned from the cell and walked towards the stairs leading back to the deck. Oshaank hurried after him.

"What should we do with it?" she asked, forgetting in her horror of the scene she had witnessed that she had more experience in this world than he.

"That is one question," Ibi agreed. "The other question is how did one of the Sheydim come to be here?"

❖

"You said you knew how to kill it," Oshaank said, gesturing back down to the hold they had just emerged from.

"I said I knew it *could* be killed," Ibiranu corrected. "How to kill it is another matter." *All things die, all things rot, all things are meat for the maw.*

"So all your magic and power is for naught? How do you expect to survive Et Adasi if you are so weak you can't kill a single demon?" Oshaank sneered, using derision to hide her fear of the thing. She was terrified more of those things would be trailing them to save their kindred.

"I was tutored in war by a god!" Ibiranu snarled back at her, his other mouths echoing *a god a god a god.* "I was honed into a weapon against these things to be used in a war almost as old as humanity. But the Sheydim are trickster spirits, and they are not a monolith. What will kill one will not work against all of them. Before I can destroy this creature, I must know more about it. Study it ..." Ibiranu trailed off. He knew war, but he knew war against humans. As much as Baal Hemodiel had taught him, he knew that the God had held back true power and knowledge. It was Hemodiel's right to do so; some knowledge was dangerous in mortal hands.

He had threatened to kill the thing and told Oshaank he needed to study it in order to do so. But the truth that was digging at his brain was that he wanted to see it again. He wanted to gaze upon its perfect form and pleasure himself as he watched the thing kill.

That disturbed him. *Why does it disturb you?* the niggling rasp of a tiny mouth inside his ear whispered, insidious tongue licking at the inner fold of his ear. It sent a shiver down his spine, but whether from repulsion or arousal, he could not say.

Ibiranu had always loved the idea of violence. He enjoyed the sparring and training; the thoughts of killing enemy soldiers and controlling their lives had a solid appeal. But to simply watch the inhuman creature, beautiful as it was, take like in a shower of gore and viscera ... that was different. Why would he want that, lust for that? He could not say—or perhaps he did not *want* to say. In the back of his mind, he worried at the mind that controlled the mouths and whispered the words they spouted. Was he becoming something other than himself? Had Ashmandai corrupted him so fully that he was now a degenerated human who lusted for Sheydim flesh in the basest of terms?

He realized he had been standing in silence, frozen by his thoughts in front of Oshaank for several minutes. She was looking at him, obviously skeptical.

"I am paying you to guide the ship to Et Adasi, not to question me, Captain," he said haughtily, covering his embarrassment with bluster.

She stared at him, her face just human enough for him to read the annoyance on it. *Kill her, eat her, find your own way, destroy them all, kill them all, own them all.* Could she hear the voices? Ibiranu didn't know, but he was terrified that they were not being whispered by the extra mouths that had opened across his body but only in his own thoughts. The near certainty that the prince of Sheydim had not only twisted his body but his very soul grew in his mind.

Ibiranu gathered himself, forcing his extraneous eyes and mouths to shut, sealing them in tight lines, allowing him to *almost* look human. He concentrated, splitting his focus between keeping his body under his control and feeling the ebb and flow of power and energy around him. It was there, invisible, stronger than it was in Carthage, perhaps stronger here than it was anywhere on the other side of these mists.

He was Ibiranu, he was the student of Baal Hemodiel, prince of Carthage and sorcerer. He would not be laid low by fear or trepidation; he would not quake in his boots over his own lusts and feelings. He was no slave to the Sheydim, and he would prove this here and now.

He opened his eyes, all of them, and marched towards the stairs, back down into the hold, followed by the gibbering chants of excitable madness from his flesh. With each step that carried him forward, he pulled more power from the world around him, sucking in power, gathering it up in his chest. He would crush the thing. If it could not be killed, it could be made to live in agony, as powerless and broken as the lowest of insects.

"God-Cursed, what are you doing?" Oshaank asked, chasing after him.

"I'm going to test the limits of this Sheyd, discover what keeps it shackled in its cell. I'm going to bend it to my will," Ibiranu answered; this time, his extra mouths answered with him, according to his mind. Focus forced control of his body. It made him feel accomplished, a euphoric sense of power and strength washing over him, bolstering his confidence.

Below deck, the Pensi were gathered in a thick throng

outside the door of the cell, hissing and shouting in their strange language. Ibi assumed they were cursing the creature. He pushed past the small Siren, shoving them out of the way, keeping an iron grip on his willpower to prevent his mutated limb from attacking and devouring any of them. Reaching the door, Ibiranu stood tall and proud, pushing, radiating all of the confidence of the prince that he was. But now was the true test.

The Pensi around him fell silent, waiting to see what would happen.

He stared into the shadows, searching out the luminescent eyes and glowing tattoos. He wanted it to watch him; he wanted it to be as intrigued with him as he was with it. He needed it; he wanted it to want him and lust after him. He placed his human hand on the cell door, feeling cool metal, seeking out the magics that held the Sheyd within. He felt nothing.

"Come then, into the light where we can see you; let me know you." He said the words softly, hoping to coax the creature into some sort of sense of safety. He saw the glowing eyes blink, but it did not move.

Yes, he wanted its affections, but failing that, he would take its fear and subservience. He let his hand drop to his side, reaching up with his malformed limb and wrapping it around the metal. He spoke with several voices issued from several mouths. "If you will not come to the light, I will bring the light to you!" he hissed.

Ibi pushed his will outward, prodding at the shadows. He wrapped his mind around the fire that sat in the lantern opposite of the cell, calling the flame.

The flame grew, writhing like a serpent, pushed out of the lantern, and extended towards the cell, pushing the shadows back as it went. The Pensi around him scattered, falling away from the living fire he was pulling from the lantern. Only Oshaank and the Sheyd seemed calm and unmoved by his small display of power.

The flaming serpent wrapped through the bars of the cell and curled in the air, growing in intensity, banishing the darkness, leaving the Sheyd bereft of cover. There in the bright light, Ibiranu admired the creature once more.

He could not tell if it was male or female. Its features were sharp, severe, but with feminine lines. Its full lips, soft and inviting, were pulled back from blood-stained teeth that were sharp and savage. Its violet eyes sat above high cheekbones, sunken and shadowed. Ibiranu ran his eyes over the figure's body; the rags let tantalizing glimpses of flesh through but hid the curves that would help him identify the sex of the thing. It was covered in gore; the bits of flesh and exoskeleton from the Pensi that it had killed stuck to its rags and flesh but did not detract from its beauty in the slightest.

Ibiranu could feel his desire swelling. It disgusted him. With a wave of his hand, he banished the flames, plunging the hallway and cell into darkness. In the moments before Oshaank found the lantern and relit the wick, the only light came from those purple orbs that stared at Ibiranu from the blackness of the cell.

Ibiranu stood reflecting on those eyes as Oshaank brought light into the hold again. He would prefer to have done this—and other things—with the Sheydim in private, but that was not to be. The Siren were too curious to resist crowding around and watching the confrontation.

"Who are you, Sheyd, and why are you imprisoned on my ship?" he finally asked.

Chapter Eight

Silence hung over the crowded Siren following Ibiranu's question. Ibi forced his breath to a slow, calm rhythm as he waited for the thing to answer. For a moment, he thought it might remain silent and stubborn, but finally, it spoke, the flash of its blood-stained teeth in the darkness a threat all on its own.

"My name is Meridiana." The voice was soft but husky, giving no indication of gender but dripping with sensuality all the same.

"Meridiana," Ibiranu repeated, committing the name to his memory.

"And what do you mean, *your ship*?" They stepped into the light, crossing their arms over their chest. "If this were your ship, I would imagine you would know who I am, why I am here. I would imagine you wouldn't be standing around with a gaggle of free Pensi staring as though you had never encountered one of my kind before."

"I have slaughtered Sheydim in the streets of

Carthage!" Ibiranu lied with a snarl. "And no matter who this ship belonged to before, it is ours now." *Ours? Mine! Mine mine minemineminemineminemine!* He forced the voices into silence.

"Have you now?" Their voice was inquisitive but mocking. "And you think I'm one of these … Sheydim?"

"I recognize your tattoos from the corpses of my foes, from the dead I've slain in service to the gods! I've seen the eyes of your prince and recognize his wicked magic in your own."

Their face turned, the smile disappearing as they stepped closer to the bars. "You call them gods, but they are petulant children with no concept of empathy. If you serve them and have looked into the face of the prince, then you, most of all, should know that your gods are naught but wardens overseeing the death of the human race through the satiation of their own lusts!"

Ibiranu started to argue but cut himself off, or at least cut off his primary mouth. His body chittered with indignation. *Lies, slander, gossip against gods! Against the ones who birthed us, who made the world in the image of the wanton; take it, fuck it, devour it, satiate your own desires as the gods would do and have you do.* He watched the Sheyd for several moments, until he could banish his doubts and take control of his flesh again.

"Simple bars don't seem enough to stop Sheydim. What holds you here?"

"Ah, that's your concern. Why haven't I escaped my cell and treated you all as kindly as I treated this meat?" The creature gestured to its gore-soaked feet and the gelatinous mass of organs and shredded flesh.

"Yes," Ibiranu answered honestly.

The creature seemed to consider for a moment, weighing its options. Finally, it seemed to have decided there could be no harm in telling him, that or it had thought of a convincing lie. "These." It lifted its wrists, revealing bracelets made of pink stone.

"Jelani magic!" Oshaank gasped. "Your powers were stolen by a Siren medusozoan mage."

"I would not go so far as to say stolen, but dampened, held in check, restricted," Meridiana corrected.

"And yet you were still able to so neatly murder the Pensi," Ibiranu mused. "So your strength and speed are intact, only your magic is hampered. So answer, truthfully, why stay in the cell and not come out to wreak havoc on your captors, on us?"

"Ending your life is not worth ending mine, Sheqez. How many of them or of you could I kill before I was overwhelmed? Many, perhaps, but I will not risk death just for a taste of your unclean flesh."

"Sheqez?" Ibiranu asked, unfamiliar with the word.

"Abomination," Meridiana whispered, the play of a smile coming back to their lips.

Behind him, Ibiranu heard Oshaank stifle a laugh. He resisted the urge to grab the crab woman and toss her into the cell with the murderous Sheyd. Instead, he let the barbed insult pass.

"And why were you imprisoned in the first place, Sheyd?"

"I told you, I am not Sheydim; I am Lillin, related, close, but not quite the same. As to why I am in chains

…" Meridiana shot a look at Oshaank. "Apparently, her people enjoy the powers of seduction and lust but are jealous and stingy when it comes to their affections."

Ibiranu had not heard of the Lillin before this moment; it made him wonder what else Baal Hemodiel had neglected to teach him. "You mean to say this is some lovers' spat?"

"I said nothing of love," Meridian scoffed.

"Politics and sex are interchangeable in Siren culture," Oshaank offered. "If they were engaging with a powerful figure—"

"I only engage with powerful figures," Meridiana interjected.

"—then it could be disastrous for certain parties. They are a political prisoner," Oshaank finished.

"I see." Ibiranu turned towards the cage. Not a Sheyd, not a Siren, Meridiana was as alien in this environment as he, and despite himself, he still wanted them, painfully. "We have no political loyalty to the Siren and no reason to keep you caged. If you'll keep your peace and not … murder any more of my crew, you may leave the cell and stay aboard as a passenger instead of a prisoner."

"God-Cursed!" Oshaank hissed, placing a hand on his shoulder and pulling him back away from the door. "That isn't wise!"

Ibiranu writhed in pain as his body fought him, trying to reach out and rip the insolent captain limb from limb, devour her sweet succulent flesh while she screamed … The images filled his mind. He pushed them down as he stepped farther from the cage. "Don't touch me," he hissed at Oshaank, struggling to control his impulses.

"Listen to me; if they're a prisoner from Althaea, especially a political prisoner, then Althaea will look for them, making us a target for all of Althaea," Oshaank argued.

"All the more reason for me to be free then," Meridiana's husky voice sounded in his ear, almost making him leap out of his skin. They had exited the unlocked cage and followed. "My strength would be needed to fight off the Siren. After all, you won't be spared for keeping me in a cell after you stole their ship, will you?"

Oshaank's mouth opened and closed, her wide, flat teeth clacking together as she struggled to think of some reason to throw the Lillin overboard, or at least back in the cell.

Ibiranu nodded. The logic was sound; the enemy of his enemy would be his ally. "If we are fortunate, we will not need to discover the extent of their ire. Oshaank, head up to the helm, get us moving in the right direction. The sooner we are out of striking distance of Rotachat, the better."

Oshaank looked like she wanted to argue, her pincer clacking as her mind raced for some excuse to re-imprison the Lillin. Finding herself bereft of reason, she turned and stalked away, heading up to steer the ship.

Ibiranu watched her go before turning his many eyes to the assembled Pensi. They required no words, fleeing under his gaze, leaving him alone with Meridiana. "Come, let's discuss the situation," he stated calmly before setting off, expecting them to keep pace. "Your quarrel with the Siren is of no concern to me, all that matters is my own mission. It is the reason we have liberated this ship, the reason we sail, the reason you are now free. Ergo, my mission is now your mission."

"And what would your mission be?" Meridiana asked, the sound of their luscious lips turned up in a smirk audible in their voice.

"I was commanded by the very gods to fetch a book, one that the Sheyd prince crafted."

"*The Book of the Children,*" the Lillin interrupted.

"You've heard of it?" he asked, surprised despite himself.

"There is no Sheyd, Lillin, or Raphamim who has not," they answered.

Ibiranu paused, looking through a doorway, exploring the ship as he considered what to ask first. This room seemed to be mostly stores, boxes and barrels stacked high and tied to the wall with heavy rope. He had not heard of the Lillin or the Raphamim before meeting them, nor had he ever been educated on this apparently infamous book until commanded to find it. He felt as though he were a newly initiated acolyte. Perhaps he was. In this new world, among creatures to whom magic was everyday instead of a miracle, he seemed woefully uneducated. It made him angry. He could feel his flesh seethe with annoyance and the desire to take it out on Meridiana's flesh.

His thirst for knowledge was all that kept him in check. No, that wasn't quite true. He still felt that hot core of lust at the center of his being. But the fact that

Meridiana held knowledge of what he was seeking, he could not pass that up.

"It has been kept a secret from mankind then. What is the book?" he asked as he continued down the hall.

"It is the magical journal of the prince. You know that much. Ashmandai crafted the book from the flesh and blood of the Nephilim Og. The foul creature's skin became the parchment, his sinew the binding, and his fiery black blood the ink. Within it, lord Ashmandai recorded his findings, magic both divine and profane. Imagine, Magus, all of the magical knowledge of the Grigori, the demonic, the Sheydim, of humanity, all in one tome."

Ibiranu was so fascinated by the concept of the book that he nearly missed being called a magus. No one had ever used that term with him before, always the student, never the master. It made his heart swell, his ego satiated. The voices along his body gibbered praise and adulation, chanting his name. He quieted all of this, trying to concentrate on his next question.

He glanced through another door, seeing a gaggle of the Pensi moving around the room. It appeared to be a mess, tables and cutlery strewn about. The industrious shrimp-men were cleaning. Ibi nodded and continued on his way.

"That makes sense," he finally said. "The gods commanded me to find the book; such magic should not be in the hands of any but them. They also claimed that the book would contain the arcane knowledge to undo what Ashmandai has done to me."

Meridiana let out a laugh, the sound as alluring as

it was infuriating. "Gods … I already told you, Magus, they are not gods, they are simply fallen servants. But what did the prince do to you?"

Ibiranu turned, distracted from their blasphemy by the question. "What do you think? I am a human, I am a man, and I look like this, twisted and corrupted by your prince's foul touch and fouler magic!"

"Oh, you deluded man," Meridiana whispered in his ear. It caused the hair on his neck to stand on end. A mouth on his shoulder opened and attempted to lick them, but they had moved away too quickly. "Sheyd magic would do no such thing. Your form is not the product of Ashmandai but of those you worship. You were shaped by them, not by Sheydim."

This was not the first time he had heard such, but the thought that his own master, his teacher, his very god had done this to him, that they had lied to him, made him sick. He didn't want to believe that. No, it was much more likely that all Sheydim, including whatever Meridiana was, were liars. They were coming to the end of the hallway; a short set of stairs leading up to an ornate door sat at the end.

"But it is true that the book could be the key to reshaping you, to returning your humanity," Meridiana finished, interrupting his thoughts. "The Grigori, those things that you call gods, claimed that with access to his magic, they could heal you, but it's the opposite. If you were to return that book to the prince, he could access their magic and heal you."

"You want me to betray my gods and hand the book over to your demon prince?" Ibi gaped at them.

Meridiana stepped past him, climbed the stairs, and set their hand on the handle of the door. "Your gods betrayed you already. You should look after yourself and those who have not." They pushed open the door, revealing what could only be the captain's quarters. Bookshelves, art, and a wardrobe all crowded the interior of the room, but Ibiranu's attention was on the way Meridiana moved to the bed, trailing their hand across the sheets. The illumination in the room, floating orbs of soft blue light, cast shadows that only enhanced their savage beauty.

"With the book, you can also free me from these damn shackles, loose me back upon the world … This is where you were hoping to lead me, wasn't it?" they asked.

Ibiranu stepped inside the cabin, shutting the door behind him but not removing his hand from the door handle. They were not wrong. He had the frustrating feeling he was being toyed with. By Meridiana, by the gods, by his own body. Voices still screamed at him, though he could no longer tell if the sound was issuing from his many mouths or just in his mind. They demanded that he stop hesitating, that he have his way.

"What are you?" he asked, barely able to quell his basest urges.

"I told you I am Lill—"

"No," he cut them off. "I mean are you a man or a woman, male or female?"

"Does it matter?" Meridiana asked, their eyes hooded, the smile playing across their lips both playful and cruel. "Besides, you're asking me this when you have yet to even tell me your name."

He paused. Something about the room, about Meridiana, he could hardly think straight. His desire felt oppressive, like he could not control himself. The voices demanded he take Meridiana by force, whispering terrible acts of wondrous lust he should enact on the creature.

"Ibiranu," he finally choked out, gripping the door as if it could hold him back.

"Ah, then, Ibiranu …" they sat on the bed, spreading their legs, giving him a view of their thighs as they leaned back on their hands, displaying a body hidden by ragged, torn clothes but maddeningly beautiful. "Come and find out for yourself what I am."

Chapter Nine

Ibiranu was roused from his slumber by a rapping on the door. He rose, wondering how much time had passed, how long he had slept, how long they had ... played. He glanced over at the bed. Meridiana was wrapped in sheets and nothing else, still sleeping. He still wasn't sure how to answer what they were, but it turned out it really hadn't mattered.

As soon as he had touched them, the voices had silenced; even now, they seemed calm and satiated. Maybe all he had needed was a solid fucking and rest. Though his body was still a twisted nightmare, Meridiana had seemed to take it in stride, intuitively understanding what his form would need for pleasure.

As he walked, he could hear the murmuring of his body waking up, the twinge of hunger, the rage, the madness, all those inhuman things that came with his new inhuman body. He ignored its demands, its calls for blood, and opened the door. Outside stood one of the Pensi, this one larger than many of the others he had seen, bright pink scars zigzagging across his carapace.

They are plentiful, kill him, eat him, none will notice, none will care. The voices came back. Ibiranu stared at the man for a few moments before shaking his head to clear it.

"What?" Ibiranu asked.

"First meal." The man glanced past Ibi into the room, and a smirk played across his mouth. "Second for you, I 'spose."

Ibiranu chuckled, unable to bring himself to be indignant. "Can you just bring the food to me?"

"Not first meal, Magus. It's bad fortune to eat alone, worse for officers to do so."

Magus, he was enjoying that title. Better than God-Cursed or sheqez, though now that he was thinking of it, he didn't know if he had ever told Oshaank his name. Not that she or any of the Pensi cared. So long as he could pay, they would be loyal. That suited him fine. But this meal might be a good opportunity to understand who he was sailing with, to learn more about the world he currently found himself trapped in.

"What is your name and station?" Ibiranu asked.

"Ah'kravat, I'm Captain Oshaank's quartermaster at present. In charge of discipline and making sure we don't get cursed for skipping first meal."

Ibiranu was suddenly glad he had not eaten the man as his body demanded. "Very well, Ah'kravat. We will attend shortly." Ibiranu stepped back and shut the door before the Pensi could say anything else. Without turning, he opened the eyes on the back of his shoulder and head. He was unsurprised to see Meridiana awake and watching the exchange.

"First meal?" they asked.

"You're familiar with the custom?"

"No, but sailors are by and large a superstitious lot, and I have worked up something of an appetite. It's not like I was being fed well in my cage before you came along."

He watched them rise, shedding the sheets as they moved to the wardrobe. Their body was perfect but defied definition, seeming to shift in accordance to shadows and desires rather than any rules flesh should follow. He stared at them hungrily as they found clothes that would fit their form and got dressed. Once most of their skin was covered, he remembered to dress himself, pulling his robes on over his head, forcing the writhing flesh of his own form to hold still.

"You can stare all you like, Ibiranu, but do not become possessive," Meridiana warned. "I belong to no one and cherish my freedom more than anything."

Ibiranu had not thought of owning the Lillin, though he had also not thought of them with others. He disliked the thought. Why should he not own such a creature? He was a prince, he would be a king, and he deserved the most enticing, the most exotic concubines to fill his harem.

"I understand," he lied. "Come, let us go and see what scraps the Pensi have found for this meal."

❖

Ibiranu could not believe his eyes. The delicious aroma of cooking meat had assailed his senses before he even reached the dining room, but upon entering, he was amazed to discover a full feast laid out upon the tables.

It was a full feast.

There were platters stacked high with sliced meats marinating in gravy. A bowl with tartare sat chilled nearby, promising incredible flavor. Most of the meat looked more tender and scrumptious than any meal he had enjoyed in Carthage, and he found his mouths watering at the thought of digging in. Steaming potatoes called his attention, sitting next to a bowl of sliced beets and glistening fowl. A leafy salad sporting carrots, yellow peppers, and tomatoes caught his eye; he had never seen food so colorful in all of his life.

Across the back table, a Pensi in an apron wielding a massive thin blade was slicing into the flesh of fish whose scales still sizzled in the oil it had been cooked in.

Ibiranu walked along the edge of the tables, taking in the sights of the food. It was unlike anything he had ever seen before. His mind came back to what Oshaank had said … this meat… this meat was the flesh of those Siren and men they had killed in taking the boat. This was a cannibal's feast. Most of the meat before him had been walking, talking, living hours before. It had been alive, with dreams and ambitions. It had been men. Perhaps he could have ignored it, pretended it wasn't so, but for one detail.

The centerpiece was a skull. It was large, too large to be human, but it was close enough that Ibiranu could guess it was one Jof the near human Siren they had killed. In fact, as Oshaank had obliterated the skull of the other, this must be the head of the man he himself had torn apart. The Pensi cooks were busy laying cooking flesh against the skull, turning it from a display piece to an edible arrangement, placing deviled eggs in the sockets to mimic eyes and strands of kelp for hair.

It should have sickened Ibiranu. But it did not.

"What are your thoughts on cannibalism?" Ibiranu whispered to Meridiana, hoping to hide his own eagerness to tear into the food before him.

"It isn't; none of this meat comes from my own kind, though I suppose it is still ghoulish." They paused, tapping their chin with a perfect finger. "But when in Ahtaea, do as the Ahtaeans do." They snaked their arm around Ibiranu's elbow and led him to a seat.

A moment later, Ah'kravat, discernible due to his scars, sat next to him. "Just waiting on the captain now," he whispered, and indeed, the activity seemed to be calming, the Pensi finding their seats.

They didn't have to wait long; the thudding of Oshaank's chitinous leg could be heard as she came down the hall to the mess room.

She pushed her bulk through the door and turned her head, looking over the table, the gathered crew, and, of course, their employer. It struck Ibiranu that this was a show, a ritual that was at least somewhat scripted, like welcoming dignitaries and diplomats in Carthage. There was a certain way to do these things.

The large woman scuttled to the head of the table and picked up a flagon, golden fluid sloshing over the side as she lifted it. "We dine on the weaker who thought themselves better," she began, only to be immediately interrupted by a cheer. She waved a hand to silence them. "But this show of strength is only the beginning of the tribulations we face. We sail above our kin and kingdom. We live life free of their rule but not of their retaliation. We choose not to separate from our origins but to connect to the sea to spite and in spite of the Kingdom." She paused, looking down into the foam of her drink, seeming to consider her next words carefully.

"Know that we sail not for some safe harbor, no succor will find us where we land. We sail for Et Adasi, the isle of flesh and death, the home of the undead. Many have tried, to be pushed back by cruel waves and gasping dead reefs. Even our kin do not approach the island, avoiding the rotting reef's jagged darkness for fear of what lies in those sunken places. We are no cowards, but are we fools?"

There was a resounding roar from the crew at the accusation.

"No, we are not. We have a map of the currents and shipping lanes; the waves will not dissuade us! We have a demon and a sorcerer of our own; let the Ahtaeans come! We will strip their flesh for our plates and feed their bones to their young! Let the putrid god of undeath himself scream for our souls; we belong to the waves and not even Merrick-Mayon himself may drag us to his darkened palace. Feast now. Each bite may be your last, but this is no change. We are the liberated; we are the free. They may try to end us, to bind us, but the sea is ours, and we'll slip to oblivion 'fore we surrender! So drink up, me hearties, and dine well, for we sail for hell!" She threw back her head and downed the flagon in several gulps.

The roar of the crew as they cheered and followed suit was almost deafening, but it was infectious. Ibiranu found himself shouting alongside the Pensi crew. Beside him, Meridiana's cruel smile was stretched almost too wide, infected by the same energy and enthusiasm that gripped Ibi. This was why Oshaank was captain. These Pensi would follow her to damnation if she commanded it—considering her speech, that is exactly what it seemed like she was asking.

Ibiranu was pulled from his reverie by a tearing sound.

All around the table, the Pensi were digging into the food before them. No one, not even Meridiana, hesitated in the devouring of the meats. Ibiranu wondered if this would be crossing a line he should not cross. A mouth tore itself open on his shoulder and laughed. *A line? A line? Was it not the line you crossed when you tore that slave girl's life from her body? When you devoured the old man for not answering you quickly enough? You live a life above your own actions … no more. NO MORE! You hunger, you take what you want. You. EAT.*

He already was, he realized. His tentacle arm was lashing across the table, grabbing great gobs of meat and food and dragging it to the mouths. Despite it being an alien appendage and acting outside his control, he could taste the food rolling across his myriad tongues. He could feel the texture of the meat as his teeth and beaks tore into it. He was eating. He looked around the table. No one was staring; as deformed and monstrous as he was, no one cared. Was his deformity so mundane in this world? He glanced at Meridiana, who was carefully cutting into a fish and daintily taking bites.

He had expected his lust to fade after he had taken them, but it had not. He still yearned to explore their body and taste everything they had to offer, again and again. *Then do it!* the voice in his ear said. *Here, now, take them on the table, penetrate them, devour their flesh, taste the entrails, drink in their soul, and wear their skin as a robe. This is eternity, they will ever be yours inside and around you.* Ibiranu gazed at Meridiana, his mind filled with images of them splayed open on the table, guts and viscera spilled out as he pleasured himself with their corpse. It was repulsive and enticing. The gibbering of his mouths reached a pitch. Pensi were beginning to turn towards him as his body reacted to his violent lust. He reached for them.

Meridian turned and looked at him, their gaze puncturing through the haze of his insanity. The image spoiled in his mind, becoming grotesque, forcing itself back to a human lust. They placed a hand on his thigh. The tendrils along his leg shifted under his robes, reaching, but their touch did something. He could feel the murderous intent wane and die down. He gasped; the emotional change was so sudden it left him breathless. The mouth on his shoulder sealed itself closed, and he found himself alone in his head once more.

What power the Lillin had over him, he was grateful for it in that moment. Whatever they were, it kept the cursed powers of Ashmandai at bay. But they claimed this was not the Sheyd prince's doing but the gods'. If that were true, why would the Lillin's touch silence it, calm it? And if it were as he had thought, Sheyd magic, what did that mean? He had the unpleasant feeling he was being manipulated, by Meridiana, yes, but also by the gods, by the Sheydim, possibly even by Oshaank and her Siren crew.

He needed to remember that he was a prince, he was a powerful sorcerer, he was in charge and in control. Every life on this ship was his to command and to let live. They survived on his kindness. He could almost feel the laughter of the voice, though it did not come back full force.

He closed his eyes, forcing his attention onto the hand on his thigh. He would need to remain calm and in control. He reached out with his human hand and lifted the wooden cup filled with wine. Opening his eyes, he raised the cup towards Oshaank in a simple toast, hiding his malicious thoughts behind a facade of civility before taking a sip and continuing the meal in a more subdued manner.

Chapter Ten

The journey, despite Oshaank's theatrical speech, was a calm one. The map provided by the gods offered the best shipping lanes to speed them along the path, and it seemed as though there would be no impediment to reaching their destination. The days were filled with Pensi going about the business of keeping the ship in good working order, while Oshaank acted as captain and navigator.

Ibiranu spent his time speaking to Oshaank, Meridiana, and Ah'kravat, asking ceaseless questions about the world he found himself in, about Ahtaea, and about the Sheydim that he had always been taught were horrifying demonic entities. While Meridiana's touch kept the murderous, ravenous voices in his head in check, Ibiranu found himself stalking the ship while the Lillin slept. He would ghost through the ship to the crew's sleeping quarters to suck the life from the sleeping Pensi.

The gibbering from his secondary mouths that seemed to form aimlessly and solely to torment him demanded that he rip the souls from the crew, devour them whole, and leave the desiccated husks in their bunks where they lay. He suppressed the urge to give in, only stealing enough from each Pensi to keep his own strength up. A little from every crew member left them feeling tired and sore but took the edge off his own agony.

Four nights into the journey, Ibiranu was standing on the deck, staring into the horizon. What was this book that the gods were demanding? Were they gods at all? From his long talks with his companions, he found the truth mired in murky myths and hearsay. The Siren had their own gods, creatures none of them had seen but all believed to be real. Oshaank accepted that the beings Ibi called gods were indeed powerful but believed them to be demigods, the children or avatars of the true gods.

That was kinder than Meridiana's view of them. According to them, the gods were nothing but spoiled children, creatures birthed from the stuff of creation who, through their own lust, fell to Earth and began fucking and enslaving humanity. According to the Lillin, the long war between the Sheydim and the gods, which they called Grigori, was one fought for the souls of humanity but along opposite lines than the ones he had always been taught.

Through his conversations with the three natives of these isles, a picture slowly emerged of a land created as an escape from the world he had known. A safe haven for the Grigori to rule and play their little games with humanity, which the true gods would strike them down for. Ibiranu did not know if that was true. He was not so ready to dismiss Baal Hemodiel's divinity at the words of a whore and a disgraced captain, but he doubted, and the voice in his head screamed those doubts in every moment of silence.

That night, as he leaned against the banister, staring out at the ocean, he felt eyes on him, a presence behind him. Without turning, he opened an eye on the back of his head and took in the view.

It was a woman. Her skin was smooth and gray and glistening with moisture, shining in the moonlight. She wore a breastplate of pink stone over her chest and a sarong of some shimmering material around her waist but was otherwise uncovered, revealing a lean but muscular form. Her hair was black and hung around her head in dark waves. Her eyes, like her hair, were a solid black, no whites or irises visible. She stood with one arm at her side, the other holding a trident, seeming completely relaxed but capable of exploding into violence in a heartbeat. Much like Meridiana, there was something intoxicatingly beautiful about her. Perhaps he just appreciated strength and viciousness.

"Who are you?" Ibi asked without turning.

"I should ask this of you." The woman's accent was strong, but he recognized it as being the same as, or at least similar to, Oshaank's. "This is a Siren ship, and you are no Siren."

"No," Ibi admitted. "No, I am not." Now he turned, allowing more eyes and mouths to open along his body as they willed, forming and closing at random. "But this is my ship."

"Taken from Siren," the woman stated.

"And by them," Ibi returned. "I am Ibiranu, sorcerer of Baal Hemodiel; you stand on my ship."

"Ash'ranu of the Kaldeni guard," she responded. As she spoke, Ibiranu saw her mouth was filled with rows of sharp, jagged teeth. Oshaank and Ah'kravat had both spoken of the Kaldeni in whispers of fear; this woman, then, was one of the shark-like Siren who made up part of the ruling class of Ahtaea. "And no, this is not your ship. No matter what happened to those you took it from, this ship belongs to Ahtaea, and I reclaim it as such."

"I think you overestimate your ability," Ibiranu whispered through a dozen mouths. *Too much talk, too little death, rip out her soul and eat it before she dies, let her watch oblivion come.*

If she was unsettled by the display, she did not show it. Her thin black lips curled into a snarl. "I think I do not, but even if I did, I would not come alone." She raised her free hand and snapped her fingers.

From all around him, he heard the sound of webbed hands scrabbling up the side of the ship.

"We're under attack!" Ibiranu shouted.

It was all he could manage before Ash'ranu threw herself at him, her trident moving at blinding speeds, faster than he could react. The tips of the weapon tore into his shoulder, popping an eye, skewering a mouth, and knocking loose teeth as it did. Ibiranu screamed in pain and lashed out, creating an explosion of force between them that pushed the Kaldeni away from him and tore the trident out. The force of the attack sent him sprawling to the deck. Several mouths howled in pain, but already the wounds were sealing.

All around him, he could see the dark shapes of more Siren pulling themselves onto the deck. He didn't care; all he cared about was killing this woman who had hurt him.

He pushed himself to his feet, set his mouth in grim smile as several other mouths along his arm began to chant the arcane words of spells. Whatever alien intelligence resided within his monstrous form, it was for once of one mind with him. He lifted his human hand as he pulled energy from the world around him, and the words of the myriad spells coalesced in shimmering runes in the air around him. A whip of boiling air formed in his hand. He gave it a crack, wielding the arcane weapon with an insane smile.

Ash'ranu struck at him again, but this time his tentacles moved at blinding speeds, wrapping around the whip and using it to block the attack. He leapt back from her, creating enough space to strike with the weapon, the air crackling as the manifest will reached out for the Siren, who rolled to the side, barely avoiding the attack.

Ibiranu did not relent, pressing the attack. He advanced on Ash'ranu with every crack of the whip, forcing her to retreat. She showed no signs of panic, her face a mask of passive concentration as she dodged, blocked, and counterattacked. She might as well have been playing some game of strategy rather than fighting for her life. Ibiranu was forced to consider that if he was not given the extra speed and strength of his deformity, he would be long dead. The Kaldeni warrior was faster, stronger, and more skilled in almost every way. Only the cursed flesh responding before he could process her attacks was saving his life now.

Around them, the battle had reached a fevered pitch. He could hear the sibilant language of the Siren spat back and forth as the Pensi crew met the weapons of their kin on the deck, the screams of anger and agonized death filling the air. A blur of violet light that moved between the isolated frenzies told him that Meridiana had joined the fight as well. They tore through those they came across, their musical laughter floating across the deck like the haunting song of the damned. Above it all, he could hear Oshaank shouting orders, a maestro orchestrating the chaos into a song that suited her.

Ash'ranu caught the whip on her trident, the metal heating and turning orange where the two weapons caught. "Two, two war criminals on your ship, Cursed-One. Two reasons to bring you and your ship down to Ahtaea, to the briny depths of our world. They will stand trial while you suffocate and drown for all time. Kept alive, kept conscious by the Jelani."

"You talk of your victory," Ibiranu hissed, pulling his whip back from her.

"I can see your exhaustion. Despite your curse, you are human; you cannot match my kind's strength, our endurance. The Kaldeni were created for war; you are just food that has gotten uppity." She stepped back and leveled her trident at him. She was not wrong about his waning strength, but she was wrong about it limiting him.

Ibi lashed out again with the whip. Ash'ranu dodged to the side, but she hadn't needed to, the whip wrapped around another Siren's throat, cooking the meat as it made contact with the surprised humanoid. Ibiranu yanked back, dragging the hapless Siren to him, his tentacles extending to wrap around his victim. Ibiranu lifted the screaming Siren in the air.

"Exhaustion? Food? No, you are food." Ibi growled as the mouths of his tentacle tore into the suspended warrior. "You are meat, you are chattel!" Ibiranu's mouth fell open, and he inhaled deeply, pulling the creature's soul from his body, sucking his strength and energy out. Ibi felt the Siren's struggles grow weaker and weaker, its skin becoming papery as he stole all vitality and strength from it. He tossed the corpse aside, turning back to Ash'ranu with a horrid smile plastered across his face.

"Gods," the Kaldeni whispered. "Three monsters, and all of you will pay." She hissed as she launched herself at him with savage ferocity.

He returned to his defense with renewed energy, laughing at the inevitability of his victory.

"Full sails, ye worthless scum! We're almost there! Send them to Mayon's grasp; let them serve in death as they forced you to serve in life." Oshaank's voice rang out. Pensi not engaged in melee scrambled to follow her orders, loosening ropes even as the combat reached new frenzied heights.

Ash'ranu continued her assault of the mage. "You mean to sail across the dying reefs. You are mad; you are all mad," she howled as she struck again and again.

Ibi laughed in response to the accusation. "Perhaps we are simply not cowards!" he spat as he used the whip to force aside a thrust.

Ash'ranu slammed her shoulder into the mage, sending him flying backwards and into the mast. The impact had shattered at least one rib. Blood ran from his mouth as he coughed, trying to catch his breath. She took a step forward, smiling, and then paused, eyes wide. Ibi stood as straight as he could and smiled, nodding at the dagger he had thrust into her ribs during her attack.

"Who is food now?" he asked through a bloody smile. He tried to lift the whip, but his arm would not respond. The magic was fading, the weapon dissolving as his strength fled. He could not show his weakness.

Ash'ranu snarled, "You are already dead. I will not join you!" She turned and darted across the ship, hand on her side, holding the dagger in place as she leapt over the side of the ship and disappeared into the gloom.

"Magus," Ah'kravat whispered, the Pensi quartermaster and two of his compatriots appearing from the chaos. He gestured for the two to help Ibi.

They moved to get under his shoulders and lift him, but as soon as they were close enough, Ibi's tentacle arm whipped out and enveloped them, pulling them down as he dragged their essence from their bodies, their squeals of terrified agony dying swiftly. The pain was excruciating as the stolen life mended his shattered ribs. Ah'kravat watched, his bulbous black eyes taking in the grisly scene without any indication of judgment.

When he was whole once more, Ibiranu nodded. "Dispose of them before the rest of the crew sees," he commanded.

Ah'kravat nodded, not questioning the order, and moved to comply.

Ibi stepped away, searching the deck with his eyes. The battle was dying down. It was obvious that the route of their commander and the bloody swath Meridiana and Oshaank had carved through the ranks of Siren had taken their toll on the Siren morale. The invaders were fleeing, swiftly leaping over the side of the ship, back into the watery depths of the ocean.

He found the glowing violet of Meridiana's eyes and approached her. "They flee us; we have defeated them," he said, satisfied; though if he were more pleased by victory or his own prowess, he could not say.

"Perhaps," Oshaank said.

"Perhaps?" Meridiana asked, eyes narrowing at the implication.

"Perhaps," Oshaank repeated as she approached, then pointed towards the stern.

Ibiranu turned his gaze to follow her claw and saw a thick fog on the water. A haunting moan seemed to be hidden somewhere within the thick clouds.

"What is that?" he asked.

"That is the Last Breath of the Dying Reefs," Oshaank answered as they entered the horrid fog. The stench of decay was immediately over powering. Visibility nearly gone. "Now we pray, God-Cursed, pray your map and our luck holds true, or else we'll join the dead reefs in their eternal damnation and service to Merrick-

Mayon in undeath."

❖

The relief that they had weathered the Siren attack soon gave way to a bottomless dread, the rot-reek of the fog laying across the surviving crew like a blanket, smothering the fire-like passion and will the Pensi had shown thus far. Even Meridiana seemed subdued, their normally glib tongue hollow and leaden. For Ibiranu, it was strangely comforting. The fog seemed to deaden the murderous screams of his body, or else he had supped on so much life during the battle it was sated. He could not say which.

As before, the Pensi had dragged the dead below deck and butchered their bodies, harvesting the meat for their feasts. But now the feasts were silent, far from the jubilant festivities of that first night.

He could not say how long they plied the waters within the fog. The stars at night were invisible, the day could not pierce the thickness of it. The only time to be kept was by the hunger they all felt and by the meals they kept.

Through it all, Oshaank stood next to the wheel of the helm, the map in one hand, a compass gripped in her claw. The way her massive appendage—which he had seen her use to crush the life out of her adversaries—delicately held the small device aloft would be comical but for the dour and humorless look on her face.

Days passed this way, then weeks. Ibiranu worried that this fog was unending, an ever-present nightmare. An eternity of lightless, joyless gray and its accompanying moans from somewhere unseen. No one was surprised when the first Pensi ended its own life. Nor the second. Each of them, Ibiranu included, had experienced the nightmares of a darkness down in the depths of the ocean, a swelling sound like a cephalopod screaming curses in its watery hell, promising to end the pain of life.

Each day, more of the crew, one at a time, sometimes in twos, would stand on the edge of the ship and slit their own throats, falling back into the embrace of the water, disappearing into the fog with only the faintest sound of them hitting water and a hateful laughter from somewhere far away.

103

Chapter Eleven

No one cheered when they broke through the fog. Fully a third of the crew had offered themselves to Merrick-Mayon, the Siren god of undeath. Oshaank called for all to join her at the helm.

Ibiranu watched the wall of fog retreating. The sun above should have been a welcoming sight, but it felt wrong, sickly, as though it was being filtered through the lens of putrefaction to reach him. Turning, he breathed in the air; the stench of decay and rot stayed with them, clinging to their clothes and skin. The island loomed ahead of them, a festering wound in the sea it sat in. He could make out dark forests of dead trees, hills, a beach of bone white sand, and further in, he could see the outline of a towering edifice, a palace of some sort, reaching from the island towards the sickly sun like a child reaching for an uncaring mother.

"This is it?" he asked.

"Et Adasi," Oshaank confirmed. "We made it."

They all stood in silence, staring at the island ahead

of them, considering what they had lost to make it, what they still stood to lose should they try to escape.

"Your gods sent you to die," Meridiana said in his ear.

"There are no gods, no masters, no power other than your own" was whispered in his other ear by something that wasn't there. The blasphemy sat oddly well with him. Comforting.

"They sent me to fetch a book," he corrected. "A book of spells powerful enough to undo the curse of my flesh, to make me my own man again." He didn't look at them, instead focusing his gaze on the approaching shoreline.

"Weigh anchor, Ah'kravat. We're close enough to shore now," Oshaank said, cutting Meridiana off from whatever retort they had been about to make.

At first, the scarred Pensi did not move, his own black eyes taking in the sights of the island they had lost so much to reach, but finally, he turned and started shouting orders in the strange language of the Siren. The crew began to move, scampering off to do their quartermaster's bidding.

"I hope it is worth it, God-Cursed," Oshaank said, turning towards him, anger plain in her human eye.

"For me, entirely," he said flatly. "And you and yours are being paid. You knew the cost and dangers of this journey before we set off, better than I did. Acting high and mighty now will do you no good. You wanted this journey just as badly as I did, more, I would wager. You will be paid, all of you, blood money on top of your fees for hiring the ship. I want you to understand, Oshaank, money means nothing to me, nothing. True power is the only currency I care about, and it will be *MINE*." This last word was spoken by every mouth opened along his body. It was a sentiment he shared with the sentience that shared his flesh.

The captain and the mage stared at one another for several moments, but Ibiranu knew that Oshaank didn't have a leg to stand on; she had indeed known the risks.

After several moments, she let out a long sigh and turned away from her employer. "We prepare the boats. Let us make for the shore; you still have to find your book, after all."

Within the hour, Ibiranu was stepping off the dinghy used to reach the shores of Et Adasi. As soon as his foot hit the white sand, skeletal hands thrust from the earth, emerging from the sand, the loam, and even from under the waves of the waterline. All around them, the undead pulled themselves from the wet earth and stood, fleshless jaws hanging agape in mute stupefaction. The four of them, Ibiranu, Meridiana, Oshaank, and Ah'kravat, found themselves surrounded by the undead.

"The living are unwelcome here." The voice was reed thin, issued from the fetid vocal chords of a corpse dressed in what had at one point been ornate and luxurious robes but were now little more than sand-clogged tatters. Small crabs scuttled from between ribs;

a long, blood red worm extended from an eye socket and back through the dead man's lips.

"The living are all around, they infest you," Ibiranu answered, annoyed. "Why should the four of us be counted different than the vermin and creatures that crawl through your entrails?"

The laughter of the thing rasped through the air like a rusty knife sawing through unyielding flesh. "At least you know your place, vermin indeed."

Ibiranu felt Oshaank and Meridiana bristling beside him, but he shook his head. "No, I merely point out the idiocy of your statement. We have come for a book, one with—"

"*The Book of the Children*," the corpse interrupted. "It has been long since any mortal set foot on Et Adasi, so long since any would brave Mayon's wall; of course you seek the book."

"The gods decreed—" Ibiranu began.

"There are no gods, no masters, no power other than me!" the corpse snarled, almost echoing the voices in Ibiranu's head. The dead crowded closer behind him. His companions unsheathed weapons. "You think to come to Et Adasi and simply take the book? I welcome you to try; I welcome you to join our ranks. We accept those torn apart as readily as those that have drowned, and we will lovingly allow you to rejoin the rest of your shipmates who, even now, walk the rotting path to the island."

The undead began pulling back, forming a path through their putrid ranks towards the island interior.

"The rest of the crew," Oshaank said. "You mean

those that—"

"Yes," the dead man answered.

"The ones who gave themselves to Mayon," Oshaank finished.

"They gave themselves to Et Adasi. Your Siren deities hold no power here. This is the unfinished corner, and no god but I sit at its throne."

"You call yourself a god, but I see nothing but a corpse," Meridiana said.

"That is all you will see, all you will be. You will not reach me alive, but as a kindness, I will keep your consciousness intact, your soul anchored to the shell of your body after your death, so you may gaze upon my true form. Will you brave the decaying forests of Et Adasi? Will you give me that sport? Or should I rip you all limb from limb here and now?" the undead monster asked.

Ibiranu wanted to strike out at the dead things, rip them apart, if for no other reason that prove his superiority. They had no life force to steal; if he should be wounded, he could not simply rip the vitality from his enemies to become whole again. To fight the army of skeletons and rotting zombies on the beach may well be possible, but would he retain enough strength to strike further into the island, to wrest the book from whatever necromancer held it?

"I think you'll find the sport is more than you can bear," Ibiranu said through clenched teeth as he held himself in check. "Come, let us see what meager horrors the master of this island can manage."

Ibi stepped forward, half expecting the multitude of

putrid remains to fall on him, but the dead stood silent and still as he walked the path they had made in their ranks. He did not turn to make sure his companions were following him, but after just a moment of hesitation, he heard the bone sand behind him crunching under their feet. At the edge of the undead welcoming party, the dunes gave way to dead, rotting trees that oozed putrid sap.

With no hesitation, Ibi entered the dead woods.

"Is everything on this island rotting?" Ah'kravat hissed in irritation, the long antennae on his face quivering as though trying to avoid the rancid smell of rotting meat that permeated the air.

"It seems impossible," Meridiana said. "Things decay. They die and then they decay. But not for eternity. The maggots come, eat the flesh, leaving nothing but bones. How long has this rotting continued? Does the meat and flesh regenerate?" she asked.

"A curse. The magic of this book you are after, God-Cursed, it's what must be causing this. Are you sure that is worth it?" Oshaank asked.

"Don't be daft, Oshaank," Ibiranu spat. "Magic is no curse. This rotting place is not a side effect of whatever magic is being worked; it is the magic being worked. Whatever being holds the book does so with this world in mind." *He has the book, you will take it, rip it from his hands, rip his hands from his arms, rip his arms from his body, rip his body apart. EAT HIM.*

Ibiranu paused, stopping to close his eyes and rub his temple. The voice was pounding in his skull, growing louder, more insistent. *There. There. THERE!* it screamed at him. He opened his eyes and saw something glinting through the dead trees. He abandoned the path they were on and made his way towards it, the voice in his head growing more and more frantic, as though a mouth had opened up on the inside of his skull and screamed the words directly into the meat of his brain.

He pushed through slime-coated leaves and discovered what he had seen, a hole in the ground, but the ground around the hole was not dirt. It was fleshy, skin with tufts of sparse coarse hair. It pulsed with breath. It was sweating, glistening with salty moisture pushed through the pores. A stale heat pushed out from inside the hole, like the breath of some unwashed giant.

Ibiranu stood on the edge of the hole staring down into the darkness. This could be a trap or a distraction. Surely the necromancer would be within the palace at the center of the island and not here, in some horrid living wound in the land. But the voice in his hand was screaming so loud he could no longer hear his own thoughts, could not hear his companions. It demanded he descend, demanded he explore this abscess of the island.

Without a word to his fellows, he followed the voice's wretched command and entered the living cave.

John Baltisberger

Chapter Twelve

Descending into the moist tunnel, Ibiranu was put into mind of the inside of a mouth. Yellowed teeth jutted from crevasses, uvula-like stalactites hung from the roof of the cave, and the floor and walls had an unpleasant give to them. Tufts of greasy hair, each follicle as thick as his wrist, sprang from irregular spaces along the wall and floor. These hairy patches acted as torches; red flames barely lit their path forward, seeming to burn the tufts without ever consuming them.

Ibiranu took all this in. It was disgusting, the smell of body odor, of sweat and piss, mingled with the stench of burning hair. But even more than that was the oppressive reek of super-heated, iron-rich blood. It grew as a miasma as they pushed forward, but Ibi was grateful none of his fellow explorers questioned him. He didn't know why he was pushing through this living tunnel other than the voices that whispered in sibilant hatred urged him on, demanding he place each foot in front of the other. It was becoming harder and harder to discern the voice of his corruption from his own thoughts.

What was intrusive, and what was intruding? Ibiranu felt as though his own features, his human features, those not twisted into a horrifying amalgamation of nightmare, would shift when he closed his eyes. He felt as though his power as a sorcerer was the only possible thing he could cling to. It scared him. He wanted to turn around and take Meridiana, here, let their soothing touch calm the voices. And if it didn't work, he could rip them apart even as they fucked.

The thought of pushing his fingers into their eye sockets, ripping their skull apart even as he penetrated them in other, more intimate but no less violent ways hardened him. The heavy odor of sweat and smegma in the cave took on an erotic note. Perhaps not a throat, but a urethra, a vagina, an anus. He reached down and adjusted his erection, giving himself a pleasant squeeze as he considered all of these things, his mind slipping from thoughts of paranoia to thoughts of sexual conquest.

These, these were not his own thoughts! He pulled his hand away from his painfully stiff penis. Violence had never been tantamount to arousal. Or perhaps it had, and he simply had refused to admit such grotesque thoughts to him. What if none of the seemingly alien thoughts were coming from his cursed flesh but rather from his own true nature? Ibiranu forced the thoughts down. No, he was not a monster; he was a good man, a prince who served his nation, who served his god.

The thought of Baal Hemodiel felt like ash in his

throat. Were the gods worth serving? Were they divine as he had been taught? Or—

His thoughts were interrupted as he saw light growing ahead, not just light, but moving shadows and the sound …

Something was breathing.

Ibiranu pushed ahead. He heard his companions grumbling, but something told him he needed to find the source.

The tunnel opened up into a cavern. While in the tunnels, Ibi had noticed a lack of the same rot that plagued the rest of the island they had seen. But here, in this cavern, the rot was present. Great swathes of bloody meat hung in gangrenous tatters from the walls and ceiling. Pus oozed from pimple-like outcroppings and pulled-in pockmarks that littered the ground. Maggots of every size, from normal to almost as big as Ibiranu's human arm, carpeted the ground. A writhing mass of life in this place of death. The light in the cavern came from its most central feature. A giant man chained to a stone obelisk in the center of the cave, his skin cracked and glowing, his hair a mane of flames.

"Nephilim …" he heard Meridiana hiss. He could hear the whisper of steel being drawn. He glanced at her with an eye that had not existed moments ago.

"What do you think you are doing?" he asked, his voice booming after the silence of their descent.

They looked at him, wide-eyed. "That thing down there, it's sheqez, beyond sheqez. It is one of the most evil things in existence; it must die," they stuttered, as though baffled that Ibiranu would not see that and agree.

He looked back down at the creature crucified in the field of maggots. It had been mutilated. Bits of skin had been peeled back and pinned to his back by long, thin silver needles to leave muscle exposed. His genitals were splayed open, carved and woven into the shape of a flower, welcoming the myriad of bloated flies that landed on him to sup on the nectar.

His testes, freed from their scrotal prison, were splayed, pierced by fine hooks attached to chains hung from the ceiling of the cavern that lifted them and kept them suspended. His nipples were likewise pierced, one still attached to his body by a scrap of skin, the other hook, having torn through the muscle, lifting the entire pectoral from his ribs.

"I do not think he is in any position to cause evil," Ibiranu murmured, stepping into the cavern. Each step was a sickening squelch of crushed and ripped maggot flesh as he approached the flaming being. Coming closer, he saw that the Nephilim's eyes were open, watching him. "Who are you? Why are you chained here?" he asked as he came closer.

"Free me," the figure answered.

"No, I think not. My companion wants to kill you, though there is a sort of freedom in that," Ibiranu said.

"Kill me then."

"Answer my questions," Ibiranu offered. "And then we may be able to free you."

"You cannot consider that request, Ibi; freeing this monster will doom us all," Meridiana growled.

"I hate to agree with the Lillin," Oshaank offered,

"but if this thing is chained here, it's probably too dangerous to be free."

"You said the same thing of Meridiana, but without their help, we would not have fought off the Siren," Ibiranu said, glancing at Ah'kravat to see if the Pensi would offer his own opinion. The shrimp-man stayed silent—just as well.

"I make my own decisions, Meridiana, I keep my own counsel, and I would have more information before I—" *Kill them all, feed them to the Nephilim and then steal his power, eat his soul, and turn his rage and power into your own.* The shouted voice echoed in the chamber. All eyes turned toward him. Ibiranu swallowed. Had that been an alien thought intruding in his mind, or his own thought invading an alien part of his body?

"We are here to undo the curse of flesh that the Sheyd prince carved into my being, not fight against creatures we have no need for. Who are you, and why are you here?" Ibiranu pushed, trying to divert attention away from his outburst.

"Curse of flesh?" The Nephilim coughed, maggots that had crawled into his mouth spilling out—how they survived the heat that emanated from the unholy creature, Ibiranu could not guess. "You spurn my fathers' gifts? Humanity does not deserve the kindness my sires waste on you."

"The gods themselves bade me come to this island, to find a book for them, *The Book of the Children*, crafted by the self-same Sheyd that twisted my flesh." *Was it the Sheyd? Or was it the so-called gods, as your walking snacks keep telling you?* "Do you know the book I speak of?"

"I know it," the Nephilim rumbled, finally answering a question directly. "*The Book of the Children. Das Buch der Kinder*, held by the necromancer Bothmal Decadis, master of this island. You will need to kill him to attain the book. I can help you; I can help your gods." The Nephilim was growing more animated. "These maggots, they feast on my flesh and blood, they crawl in patterns, weaving arcane symbols and sigils with their movements and my vitae. It keeps the gods from this place, hides it from them, wards it from them. If you free me, that falls away, and the gods will reward you in ways you cannot even imagine."

"Magic to ward against the gods," Ibiranu whispered. "How could such a thing be possible?" *The gods are just another force to contend with, the gods, with the good, with this meal you are a god, you create a kingdom in your image, why be a prince when you can be god?*

"It's possible because he is their flesh and blood," Meridiana said. "The Nephilim are the get of the Grigori, the horrid offspring, product of the fallen ones taking humans by force and twisting their flesh into disgusting shapes that could survive carrying one of these monsters to term. Like repels like; we kill this wretched thing, get the book, and we can flee to East-of-Nod before his daddies show up."

Meridiana reached out and wrapped a hand around Ibiranu's bicep. The calming effect spread through him, but the thoughts were lodged in his brain, they no longer seemed alien. "We can kill him and be free," they were saying, almost pleading with him.

"No," Ibiranu finally managed, pulling from their

grasp. "No," he repeated. "I do not need your help; I do not need the gods." *They aren't gods, they are vermin, all of them, everything will be beneath me when I have the book. Kill them all, eat their flesh, become ascendant.* "We leave him here to rot and keep us free from his fathers."

"Wait! Why, why won't you kill me? You say you came here in service of the gods; why do you not serve them now and bring them here?" the creature wailed, struggling against his bonds, which only tore at his flesh more, weakening him further.

Ibiranu stepped closer, crushing maggots as he moved. "Because they are not gods. Because they are something else, something that has lied to me my entire life and twisted me into this abomination!" Ibiranu screamed the last bit of accusation. The heat of creature's skin was blistering, making his eyes water. *Gods are made. Godhood is claimed.* "You suffer for the sins of your father. And I will add their sins against me to your sentence. As long as they live, so, too, will you."

Ibiranu spat in the face of the flaming giant, saliva sizzling and evaporating in seconds. "I will kill you when I have finished with them." With that, Ibiranu turned and marched back the way he had come, passing by his bewildered looking companions.

Meridiana hurried to keep pace with him. "That's it then; you're joining our war against the Watchers?"

"I make my own war. I will not serve as anyone's pet. Not anymore," Ibiranu answered, not looking at them.

"A war against Rotachat is not a war you can win," Oshaank said as she scuttled to catch up with them.

"If you are too much of a coward to join in a war

against them, then go back to Ahtaea and serve your masters there. Up here, you must choose a side, Oshaank. Will the free Siren continue to fight for freedom or trade one servitude for another?" Ibiranu no longer spoke through one mouth. The intrusive thoughts and his own were indistinguishable, and he spoke as a choir, an alien reverberation to his tone.

"The human gods leave us well enough alone," Oshaank stammered. "It is not bravery to—"

"It is cowardice to not!" he snarled, not letting her finish her thought or statement. He was tempted to turn and rip her head off, literally, to tear into the hole in her neck and pull out the meat of her to eat. Siren was an acquired taste, and she herself had made sure he had eaten enough to acquire the desire for more. He took a deep breath. "You can stand with me, you can stand aside, but if you stand against me, you will find me a terrible enemy, Oshaank."

"Ibi!" Meridiana chastened him. "This is his doing; this necromancer, or the Nephilim, they set us against each other so we kill ourselves before ever reaching him. Do you want the book, or do you want to make enemies out of friends?"

He watched them speaking with fourteen eyes that opened and closed along his body. He needed to sup on life to push down the change, and everything but his companions on this island was dead. He doubted he was strong enough to resist the screaming urges of his flesh. But that doubt made him furious, gifting him the resolve to push down his basest instincts.

"The sooner we have killed this necromancer and

have his book, the sooner we can quit this place," Ibiranu whispered through clenched jaw. "Come, let us finish this." He continued walking towards the mouth of the cave.

121

Chapter Thirteen

They emerged once more into the dead woods, the smell of rot replacing the overpowering stench of cooking blood. It was almost a welcomed change. The night air was cool, and for a moment, Ibiranu felt relief, as though exiting the cave alone was enough to grant him succor from the curse of his flesh and growing madness.

"We should have killed it," Meridiana said, ruining his moment of peace.

We should kill them. "Should we have, Meridiana?" he asked. *They question our every move, their corpse will be as pleasing as their living flesh, no reason to keep allowing them to question us, to harangue us with doubts.* "And tell me why you think revealing our location to the—" He paused. Not gods, what had Meridiana been calling them? *Grigori.* Mouths lining his ribs spat the word with more venom than he could have imagined. "Grigori … is a good idea. Tell me, would doing so benefit us in anyway, or would we simply be opening a path for Refesh and Shadrap to come and claim the book for themselves, leaving us stranded?" *Stranded! Unloved, twisted, better twisted than a servant!*

Meridiana didn't seem to have an answer to that, so they pulled their coat tighter over the corset they wore and said nothing.

Oshaank shook her head. "The madness of your god-curse is devouring you, Ibiranu. Your thoughts aren't your own, not if you think to challenge not only this necromancer but your gods as well."

Ibiranu snarled at her, a guttural gurgle of rage, then turned too many eyes to Ah'kravat. "And you, what is your opinion on all of this? You stay strangely silent, Pensi."

Ah'kravat looked surprised to be asked, as though any being seeking the thoughts of a Pensi was an alien concept. He clasped his tertiary hands together before him, the shell of his exoskeleton clacking as he did so. "The Pensi are not cowards. The humans treat us no better than the Siren courts; why should we serve the interest of any kings of gods? I say take the book, and to Mayon's abyss with the rest."

"Ah, at last, reason," Ibiranu purred. "Words spoken unclouded by the fear of a coward or the passion of a revolutionary." He rolled his eyes towards the palace that towered over the island, visible even through the dead trees. "Our companions, Ah'kravat, seem to lose their nerve, their zeal on the last leg of our journey, when victory is so close."

"I am not losing my nerve, Ibi; I worry that you lose your focus," Meridiana protested.

"I am as focused now as I am ever," he muttered,

distracted by the images of victory and power flooding his brain. "I see the road before me; I know the path to take. And every moment we stand here, whining about those paths not taken, is another minute we give our quarry to prepare for us."

All were silent. Perhaps Meridiana or Oshaank thought he was losing his mind, but his words rang true. Wordlessly, they resumed their ascent towards the palace of the necromancer.

The woods gave way shortly after they left the cave of flesh, replaced by bone outcroppings of crucified skeletons. The condemned corpses were crowded so close that the group was forced to walk single file and pick their path through the bone strewed ground. Here, at last, they saw an end to ceaseless decay. Nothing moved, no maggots feasting on flesh, no rats picking through putrid meat; only the clatter of sunbaked bone crumbling under their feet and the soft howling of a constant wind made any sound.

"For all his bluster," Ibiranu said as he pushed through the winding bone path, "we have not seen a single obstacle in reaching this necromancer. An army of the dead on the beach and not a single walking corpse since. I am beginning to think he is all bluster. Perhaps he is unable to even control the dead more than making them speak." He paused to examine one of the skeletons. Held together by dried sinew, the thing looked as though it were howling at the sky. It was human in almost every way, but for some odd growths of bone, as though the corpse had sported horns and spines in life. He noticed that the bones of its fingers had been sharpened, as if to make them into claws.

"We should be grateful for the lack of resistance," Ah'kravat agreed. "If this is all he can muster, then we will have no problems wresting the book away from him."

"You are overconfident," Meridiana chided. "An unseen threat is no—"

She was cut off by a strangled scream. Above the field of skeletal remains they were pushing through, a ghastly figure floated. It looked like a woman who had been ripped apart in much the same way the Nephilim had, torn apart by hooks and chains.

As it continued its abyssal howl, it was joined in the sky by more and more glowing apparitions. Each ghostly figure added its own voice to the aural assault, and just through the wall of sound, Ibiranu could hear words forming. *You kill not for life but for pleasure. The old man, the serving girls. You pretend this is new, you pretend this is a curse; you hungered before you came here, before you were changed!* Each accusation spat by the spirits landed home in his soul, puncturing him with the truth. They were words that had been whispered often enough by the mouths his cursed flesh sprouted, they were thoughts that intruded on his meditations, and now they were laid bare for all the world to hear.

The four companions stood amidst the bones, unsure how to prepare for this sudden threat. The sky was filled with the spirits, as full as the field was with skeletons. The terrible realization struck Ibiranu first.

"Run." He didn't wait to see if they followed his order; he simply started running. As soon as his first panicked footstep fell, the ghostly host fell upon the field. Each and every soul that had joined the unholy choir of screams and accusation found a home in one of the skeletons. A terrible light filled empty sockets, and the corpses began to pull themselves together, freeing themselves from the crucifixion that had held them in place.

Skeletons rose before him, reaching with knife-like claws, eager to tear his flesh from his bones. Ibi dodged to the side, the claws scraping his arm, drawing ragged lines of red blood across his flesh. The wailing of the banshees, the constant storm of accusations shouted into the winds, was a cacophony. It drove him forward in a panic, emptying his mind of spells or reason. He glanced back to see his companions scrambling through the bone field behind him. From the expressions on their faces, they were likewise afflicted.

The dead surrounded them on all sides, their teeth and claws reaching out, all filed to vicious points, snapping, scraping, screaming. Ibiranu lashed out with tentacles, his mutated arm wrapping around the dry corpses and tossing them, mouths forming to crush femurs between beaks or fangs before they disappeared once more into his flesh. Oshaank's shell and Ah'kravat's exoskeleton protected them from the worst of it, but Meridiana was not faring well, their clothes torn, their body bleeding from innumerable wounds.

They all pressed forward, Oshaank doing her best to

shield Meridiana from the relentless attacks. "There are too many of them!" she shouted.

"I see that, Oshaank!" Ibiranu roared back, straining to be heard over the sound of their tormentors. "Unless you have something constructive to add?" he asked, ducking under the swipe of something terrible. Had it ever been human? Maybe the banshees didn't care about form. As they pressed forward, more of the skeletons had too many arms, too many heads, bone configurations that, if given muscle and skin, would seem too outlandish a form to ever survive.

"We have to get to the palace, to get inside!" Meridiana screamed as a chunk of meat was ripped from their shoulder. Oshaank bent over the smaller Lillin and used her sword to fend off the creatures.

Perhaps if any of you were helping me clear a path, Ibiranu thought as he turned his attention back to the monsters ahead of him. While his own mind was incapable of forming the complete and complex thoughts that would allow him to use sorcery, his cursed flesh had no such limitation. He was shocked to find his tentacle arm weaving familiar arcane sigils in the air. It left a trail of sapphire flames in the air, carving the symbol in reality. More than that, the glowing lines of flame seemed as such to the floating banshees, drawing them into the fire and absorbing them, using their essence to power the magic being woven into it.

Ibi fended off another skeleton, this one little more than a skull that used a myriad of ribs as legs to scuttle across the battlefield, and then gasped for breath. A mouth opened across his chest, tearing open the flesh to reveal ribs, muscle, and bone beneath. Teeth like gray tombstones bit at the air before a lolling tongue formed. It was agony. The cursed orifice stretched at his untainted skin, as though to claim more ground for his deformity, but it only grinned and uttered a string of jumbled arcana.

A beam of unimaginable bright white light surrounded by crackling sapphire energy blasted from the sigil his limb had drawn in the air, easily six feet in circumference and extending almost all the way towards the palace. The beam cut through the skeletons, leaving smoldering ash in its wake. The wailing lessened as even those damned ghosts without bodies seemed caught up and devoured by the light. Ibiranu reached up, directing the beam like a conductor. He would let the spell devour every soul on the island to power the beam that would destroy every corpse or life that challenged him. He swept the spell across the battlefield, leaving a swathe of burning ash behind.

Slowly, the spell sputtered out, costing more in energy and will than it was able to rip from the now fleeing banshees. Ibiranu dropped his arms. He felt drained by the spell, though it had been cast not by him but by the curse that inhabited his body. Was that true, though? Was the curse separate from him? More and more, Ibi felt as though the curse only tapped into what was truly within him, trapped deep in his dreams and nightmares until given flesh.

Though the spell had given them time and a path, the undead still advanced; the banshees had retreated, but still the skeletons advanced.

"Go!" Ibiranu demanded, beginning his dash once more.

With a cleared line to the palace, he could see the towering doors ahead. The other three were scrambling as fast as they could behind him; they all knew he wouldn't manage another spell of that magnitude immediately. If they were surrounded again, their bodies would join the field of bone and gristle that guarded the palace.

They picked their way across the field of ash, the bony assailants closing in. Ibiranu did not dare take the time to look back again. The wailing of the damned had stopped, replaced by the eerie sound of bones moving across each other, a terrifying sound amplified by the sheer magnitude of numbers. He simply ran, fleeing as he had fled a lifetime ago when he first saw the Sheydim in Carthage.

Run run run run run eat eat eat eat eat. The chant powered through his skull. He needed to replenish his strength; he needed to steal the life of another.

As he ran for the doors of the palace, his mind played over his three companions and who he would need to kill first to ensure his own survival. It wasn't until he reached the massive doors and turned that he realized the sound of the dead had stopped. Their pursuers had fallen still. They stayed a good 30 yards away from the palace, forming a perfect hemispherical line around them. It was jarring to see how close the horde had come to absorbing and consuming them.

Ibiranu panted, trying to catch his breath, and saw his companions in similar state. He half expected one of the damned to step forward, to once again hear the monolithic monologue of the egotistical monarch of this place, to be mocked before the horde of dry assailants descended on them.

But no speech came.

No sound at all. The undead army, and it was an army, was arrayed before the palace like a statue garden of death and decay, a monument to the way of all flesh. Ibiranu swallowed, gathering his wits before turning away from the army and placing a hand on the door of the decrepit palace. The wood was cool to the touch, dry as any of the skeletons, with clear signs of rot. He pulled on the rusted iron loop, and slowly, the heavy wood door swung open with a protesting squeal from unoiled hinges.

Light from inside, from sputtering orange torches, spilled out, lighting the gloom and casting dancing shadows across the backdrop of undead. The foyer just inside the door was moldering with rotting rugs and blackened painting devoured by fungal growth. A hall led deeper into the fallen domicile, lit by torches that flickered in the draft from the open door.

"It appears we are expected," Ibiranu whispered, trying to force more steel into his voice as he stepped into the palace of the necromancer.

131

Chapter Fourteen

Ibiranu walked the halls, head held high as he traversed the decayed ruins of the palace, followed by the Lillin and two Siren. He considered himself, how changed he was by this endeavor. Only weeks ago, he had been running through the streets, green to real combat, as Rome invaded his home. Beyond legends and stories, he had never seen supernatural creatures, never faced the monstrous. Now he *was* the monstrous. While the curse deformed him, while it scratched at his brain and built a terrible hunger for blood and death in him, it also seemed to strengthen him. It had kept him alive and magnified his power ten-fold if not more.

With that in mind, it made sense why he had been molded in this form by Baal Hemodiel. Only by increasing his lethality and power could he hope to stand toe to toe with the Sheydim. The rest, though, the rest was clouded. He still did not understand why Baal Hemodiel would send him here, why Refesh and Shadrap would have lied, not just spoken the truth, why they wouldn't fix him. *We need no fixing, we need no changing, we are perfection, we are power.* The gibbering of the extraneous mouths broke the silence of their egress, but Ibiranu ignored them.

The answer was clear. They did not heal him because it did not suit them to do so, not when they could send him after the book instead. Ibiranu's lips curled away from his teeth in a silent snarl; the so-called gods were using him. All in a bid to get this book. *What does a god taste like? What will they say as you tear their flesh and eat their bones? Marrow of divinity slides down the throat so sweet!*

"Ibi?" Meridiana asked, placing a hand on his human shoulder.

Their touch banished the scratching of the voices and pulled him back to the present. He realized two things in that moment. The first was that they were no different than the gods, using him to get to the book, to win it for their prince. He pulled his shoulder from their grasp. The second was that they were no longer alone.

They had emerged from the hallway and into a large throne room. An audience chamber of sorts. Tattered tapestries celebrating long dead kings and victories lined the walls, worm-eaten and threadbare. Everywhere the eye looked, across the walls, floors, and what furniture had survived, words and symbols had been scratched in the stone. The words and shapes swirled in Ibiranu's vision, painful to look at.

Perhaps at one point, this room had been opulent, but now it had fallen into disrepair. This would be the sort of room Ibiranu would have expected to find their terrible host in, languidly sprawled in the throne, waited on by the dead. Instead, the ragged old man trembled before the quartet of invaders in the center of the room.

His skin was gray, matching the old and nearly useless robes he wore. One bony, wrinkled, and trembling hand was raised as though to fend off their advance. The other clutched a massive book to his breast.

It is there. That is the book, Das Buch der Kinder, that is power, that is the reason for all of this.

Ibiranu stepped back, ready to throw up some sort of defensive spell to deflect whatever spell the necromancer would throw at them, but no spell came.

"Please," the necromancer pleaded. "Please leave me alone, I … I will let you go; I won't stop you. I'll even part the mists … please."

"The book," Ibiranu said, his eyes locked on the tome. He needed it; he could feel a yearning for the book that outpaced any desire he had ever felt before. More than he had felt for Meridiana or any courtesan back in Carthage. He was aroused by the book, drawn by it, owned by it.

With this book, we will kill them all, take our place as one of the true masters.

"Yes," Ibiranu agreed. "Give me the book."

The necromancer seemed almost surprised to find the book in his arms. "My book? But … it's mine …" He snapped his gaze back up at Ibiranu. "It's mine!" he shouted, his hand ceasing its trembling.

Ibiranu was on the necromancer before he was even

aware he was moving, wrapping the man up in his tentacles, prying the book from his grasp. "I am almost disappointed," he growled as the old man screamed in pain. Mouths opened along Ibiranu's limbs and bit into the man, tearing into his flesh. "I had thought there would be some grand duel, a battle of wills and magic, and instead, you are already defeated."

"Yes, defeated," sobbed the necromancer. His pathetic warbles disgusted Ibiranu. "But you need me … you can't … you can't read the book without me!"

Ibiranu paused, ceasing his devouring of the man's still living flesh. "What?"

"It's not in any language man was meant to know. For years I've been translating. All this you see around you is my notes, in my own cypher. Without me, the book is useless to you."

"It won't matter; we're returning the book to the gods," Oshaank growled. "Kill him."

"Not in a language of men? So it is written in the language of gods …" Ibiranu mused.

"No," Meridiana said. "It was not written by the gods but by Ashmandai himself." They reached out to touch the book but stopped themself. "It is written in the language of old earth, of creation and the Sheydim. I should … I could read it."

Ibiranu glanced back at the necromancer, suspended in the air by Ibi's grasp. "Then it seems your last hope is spent." Ibiranu did not wait for the old man to respond. He ripped him apart, pulled and gnashing through the skin. One tentacled tore into his belly, spilling his intestines across the floor; two more tentacles formed from the flesh of his limbs, ending in lamprey like mouths, and set about devouring the entrails. All the while, the necromancer continued to scream. Ibiranu brought the book to his human hand; the tentacles were not acting on their own, not anymore. They were not an invasive will, they were his.

He took one last look at the screaming mage as he was ripped apart physically. It was a cold joy, but he was hungry, so hungry. He stepped forward, closer, his feet splashing in the viscera beneath the necromancer. Lowering the man, Ibiranu leaned close, placing his mouth over the old man's eye socket and sucking. The man's screams reached a fevered pitch as Ibiranu pulled the man's eye out of his skull and crushed it between his teeth. He kept inhaling, drawing the man's soul out and swallowing it.

The necromancer's struggles grew weaker and weaker until Ibiranu had stolen every ounce of his essence and tossed the corpse aside.

"Begin translating," he ordered Meridiana, offering the book to them.

"No, we, we should return this to Ashmandai. With it, we can punish the Grigori, we can heal you," they protested.

"I do not need healing!" he roared through a dozen mouths. "Now begin translating!"

"And if I refuse?" They crossed their arms under their chest, their eyes, so alluring and strange, glowing brightly.

Ibi still wanted them, yearned for them, but he needed the book more. He needed to know what it said; he needed its power. His attack was so sudden that Meridiana couldn't process what was happening until it was too late. He lashed out with his tentacles, slamming the Lillin into the ground. He stepped close and placed a hand on their head. His thoughts pushed into their skull, not gently.

They screamed in agony as Ibiranu tore at them. His mind, bolstered by the power of his curse, screamed in her skull. "You do not have to do so willingly. But you will do it. This power will be mine, and mine alone." He pushed their head into the floor, grinding their flesh against the coarse stone. "I will not give it to your mongrel prince. Human, Siren, all of us will be free, as I will make war against all the gods, *all of them, until nothing is left to worship except me.*"

"Enough of this madness!" Oshaank shouted, leaping towards Ibiranu, her sword high in the air. He turned and saw death's approach. To be so close to victory and to be struck down …

There was a flash of steel, and Oshaank's momentum was suddenly arrested. She stood looking confused for a moment, lifting her hand to her throat, where a thin red line opened and began pouring her blood across her chest and to the floor. She turned to look at Ah'kravat, which caused the wound to tear further. Blood pooled beneath her as she collapsed to her knees.

"Freedom, a new home for exiles, you are too blind and proud to see it. You would give the book to the gods? To human gods who would as soon see us enslaved again? I won't allow that." He spat in Oshaank's face as the Siren captain gaped, trying to mouth words. But they wouldn't come out. All that was left was a few meager drops of blood, and then not even that.

She fell forward, face first, splashing in the puddle of her own spent life.

Ah'kravat turned to Ibiranu. The Pensi was tense, he could feel the sword of Damocles above them. He had thrown in his hat, chosen a side, and now was at the mercy of Ibiranu's sanity and ego.

"You chose well, Ah'kravat. We will build a new kingdom here, a stronghold to end the petty tyranny of beings who deserve no power. You will be my right hand." He glanced down at the still screaming Meridiana. "And with time, you will realize your place. You will join me willingly, as slave or consort, I do not care, but you will serve." He rose and began walking towards the back of the throne room, carrying the book clutched to his breast. Behind him, he dragged the now weakened Meridiana in the embrace of his tentacled limb.

"Come now," he told his companions, willing and not, "let us explore our new home."

Epilogue

2022 CE

For weeks, the armada had pushed through Mayon's wall, the dense fog that surrounded the mythical island of Et Adasi. It was not the first to do so, but the crew of the *Kamdiel's Demise* hoped it would be the last. A full battalion of soldiers, armed to the teeth, complimented by mages and even several Siren sent by Ahtaea to bolster this effort, stood on the deck of the ship as the island came into view. It loomed in the fog-shrouded waters like a boil pushed up from the sea.

Gime Torak, warrior cleric of Shadrap, stared at the island where the monster made its lair. He had grown up on tales of the vile mage who had stolen knowledge from the gods in order to form his own kingdom. But seeing it here, solid and real, was terrifying.

All around him, the warriors of Rotachat and Ahtaea were silent, taking in the sight of the bustling city and gleaming palace that dominated the center of the island. They passed dead ships of every sort, Siren, Human,

Gods. Each one bore the signs of terrible violence and the corpses of their crews crucified to the masts and banisters. A warning given far too late.

"Gods," Gime swore, watching the island grow closer. "It's all true."

"Less true than you might assume." The choir of voices spoke in unison; they were male, female, and some that defied all hints of humanity.

Gime started to turn, but before he could, a mess of tentacles wrapped around his chest, pinning his arms to his side. Pulled from the deck, he was turned so that his assailant could look at him and he at the assailant.

His face was half human, almost beautiful in a way, but the other half was a knot of writhing tendrils and eyes, mouths that seemed to form and then fade even as Gime watched. There was no mistaking this monster, whose name was whispered by mothers to force their children to finish their chores.

"Fleshcrafter …" Gime whispered.

"If you insist," Ibiranu agreed.

The sorcerer pushed his power into the flesh of the cleric, warping his body, reshaping it. Muscle swelled, splitting skin even as Gime's bones twisted and grew, forcing claws out of fingertips and tusks through his lips. The Fleshcrafter warped the flesh more and more until what was once a man resembled his right half, a shambling mound of mouths, eyes, tentacles, teeth, and claws. He set the newly made monster down.

"Spread your joy," he commanded.

Gime's human eye widened in fear, what was left of him trapped now by Ibiranu's will. His body turned from the sorcerer and charged into battle with Gime's former brothers in arms. Everywhere the monstrosity struck, it spread the sickness of flesh, warping body and mind with every blow. All around them, the exiled Siren rose from the waters, bringing the battle to those who thought to invade their home.

In two thousand years, no aggressor had managed to reach the shores of Et Adasi. Their mutilated corpses would be left on display for all to see. Those who survived, changed, would walk the ocean until they found Ahtaea or some island settlement to spread Ibiranu's corrupting influence.

The Fleshcrafter walked to the edge of the boat and gazed at the island he had transformed. Thoughts of the home he'd had, of Carthage, had long since faded. It was no longer important to him, though he doubted it survived still. It didn't matter, all that mattered was reshaping the world, crafting it into one that would be pleasing in his sight.

143

John Baltisberger

John Baltisberger is an award-winning author of speculative and genre fiction that often focuses on Jewish Elements. Beyond his writing career, John is the Publishing Editor of Madness Heart Press, Madness Heart Games, and Aggadah Try It.

A fan of transgressive and experimental literature. He lives with his wife, daughter and trash-goblin/pug Beans in Austin, Texas. You can see his work and more at www.KaijuPoet.com

More Books from John Baltisberger

From Madness Heart Press;

UPD, Texas Case Files: 1.1-1.3
978-1-955745-01-7

From Aggadah Try It;

Book of Ze'ev: Treif Magic
978-1-7348937-0-0

Book of Ze'ev: Son of the Right Hand
978-1-955745-04-8

From St. Rooster Books;

Abhorrent Siren
978-1-955745-02-4

Aborrent Faith
978-1-955745-09-3

Blood & Mud
979-8647568397

From Death's Head Press;

War of Dictates
978-1-7348937-1-7

More Kaiju Press Publications;

Bel the Last Dragon: Jungles of Habbiel
978-1-955745-18-5

Stabberger Season One
978-1-955745-12-3

The Subjective Truth of the Esoteric Mind
978-1-7348937-2-4

9 781955 745369